D1408325

FAR OUT
FAIRY TALES

STONE ARCH BOOKS
a capstone imprint

INTRODUCING...

HANSEL & GRETEL

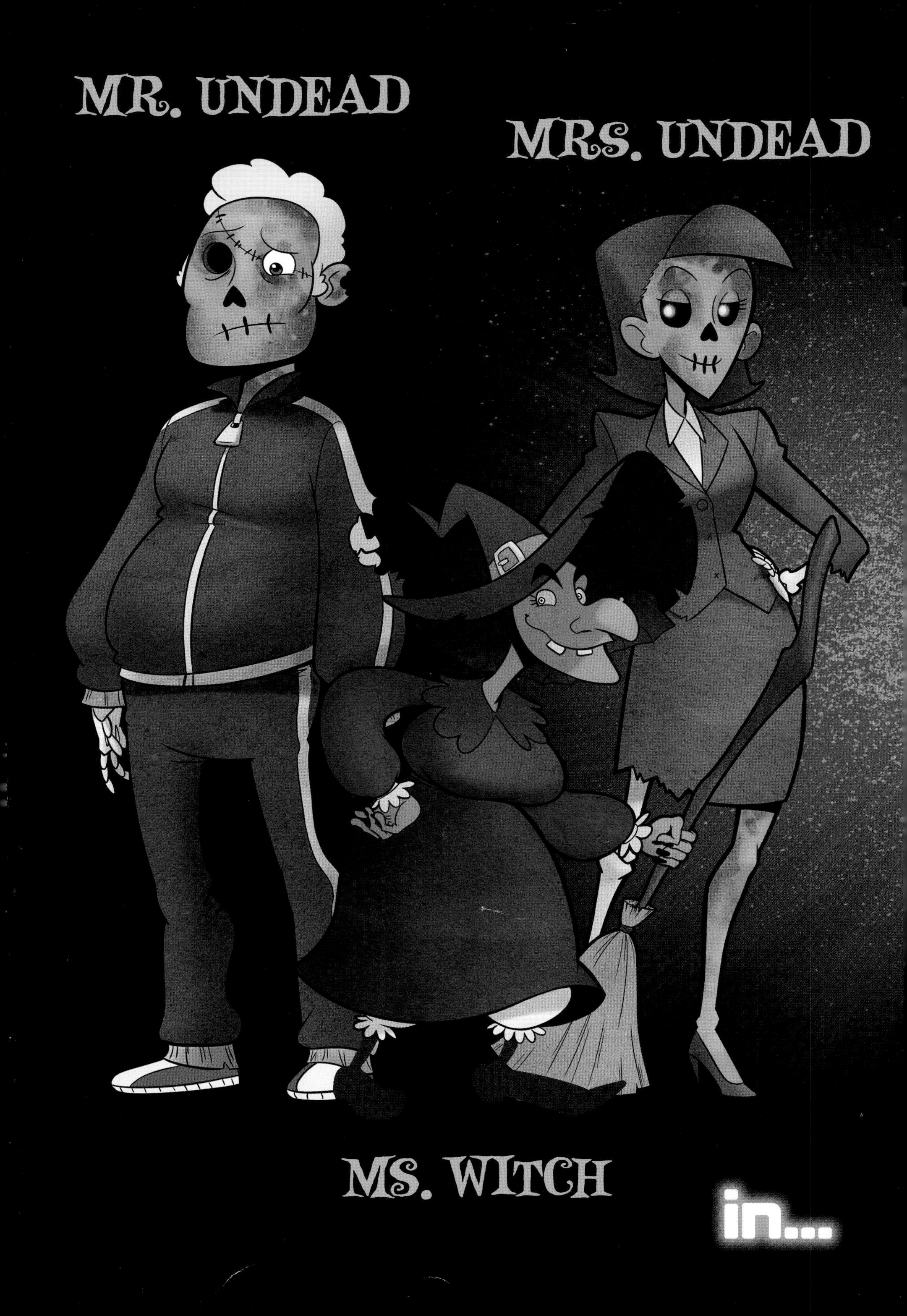
MR. UNDEAD
MRS. UNDEAD
MS. WITCH
in...

Far Out Fairy Tales is published by
Stone Arch Books
A Capstone Imprint
1710 Roe Crest Drive, North Mankato,
Minnesota 56003
www.mycapstone.com

Cataloging-in-Publication Data is
available at the Library of Congress
website.
ISBN 978-1-4965-2509-3 (Hardcover)
ISBN 978-1-4965-3115-5 (paperback)
ISBN 978-1-4965-2512-3 (eBook)

Summary: The Undead Family is out of
brains to eat! Tourists have stopped
visiting their home--a graveyard--for
some time now, and the zombie family
is starving. So they venture into the
Magical Forest disguised as tourists,
hoping to lure humans to an early
grave! Unfortunately, an evil witch
has other plans for the crepescular
kiddies . . .

Designed by Hilary Wacholz
Edited by Sean Tulien
Lettering by Jaymes Reed

Printed in US.
062016   009823R

FAR OUT FAIRY TALES

HANSEL & GRETEL & ZOMBIES

A GRAPHIC NOVEL

BY BENJAMIN HARPER
ILLUSTRATED BY FERNANDÓ CANO

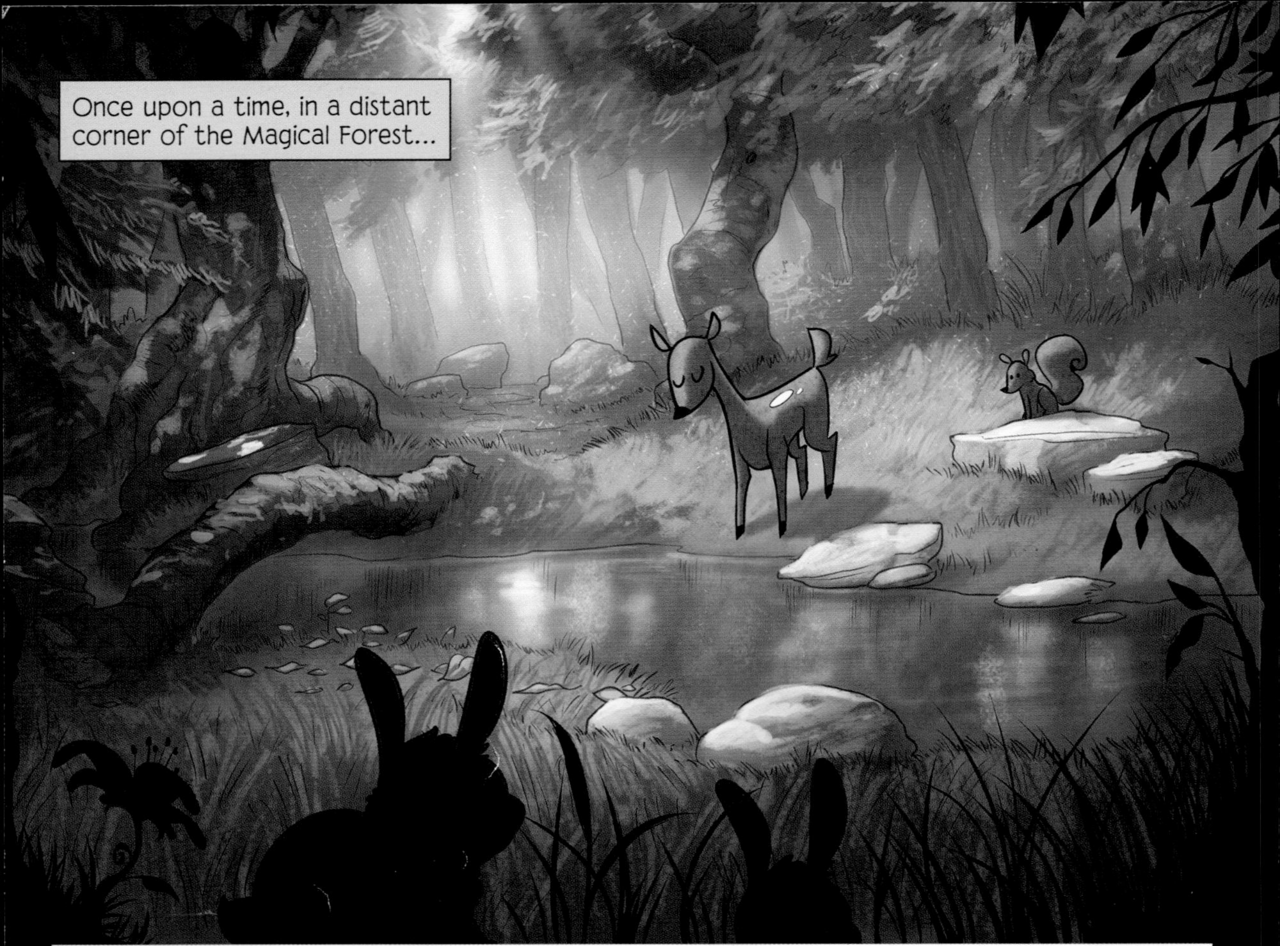
Once upon a time, in a distant corner of the Magical Forest...

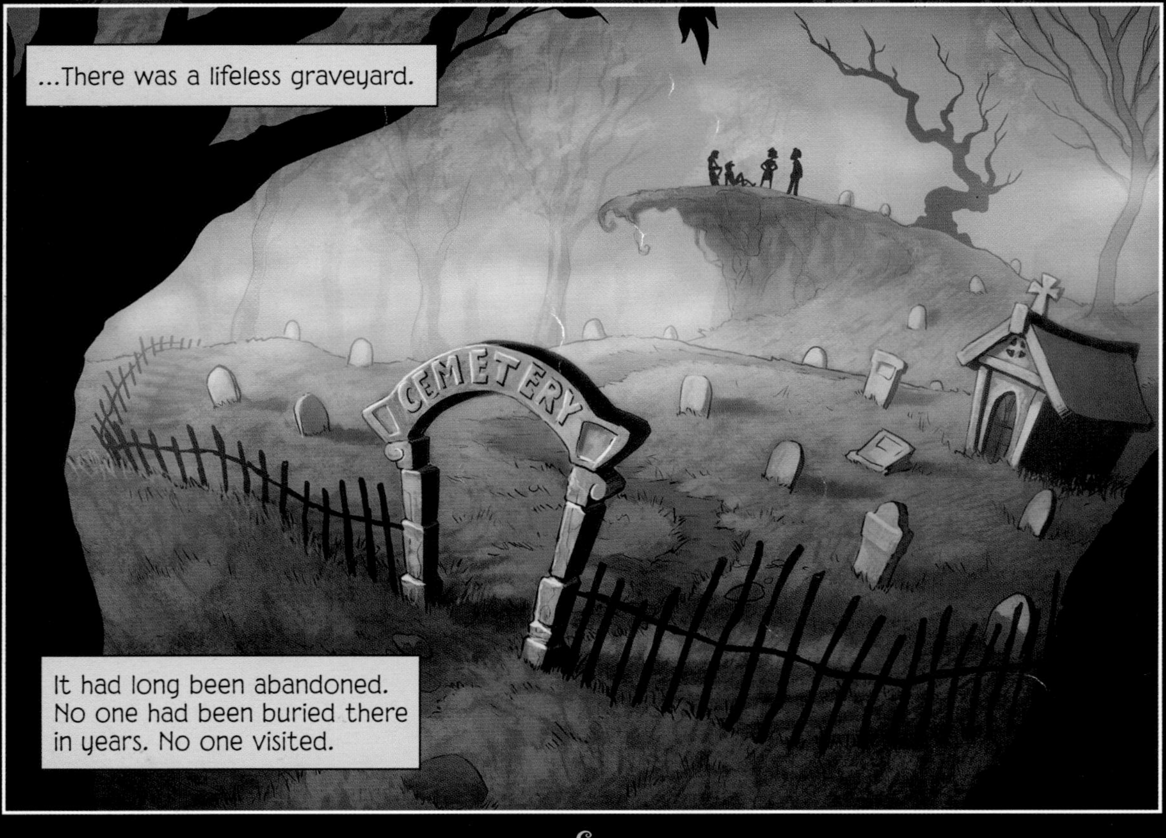
...There was a lifeless graveyard.
CEMETERY
It had long been abandoned. No one had been buried there in years. No one visited.

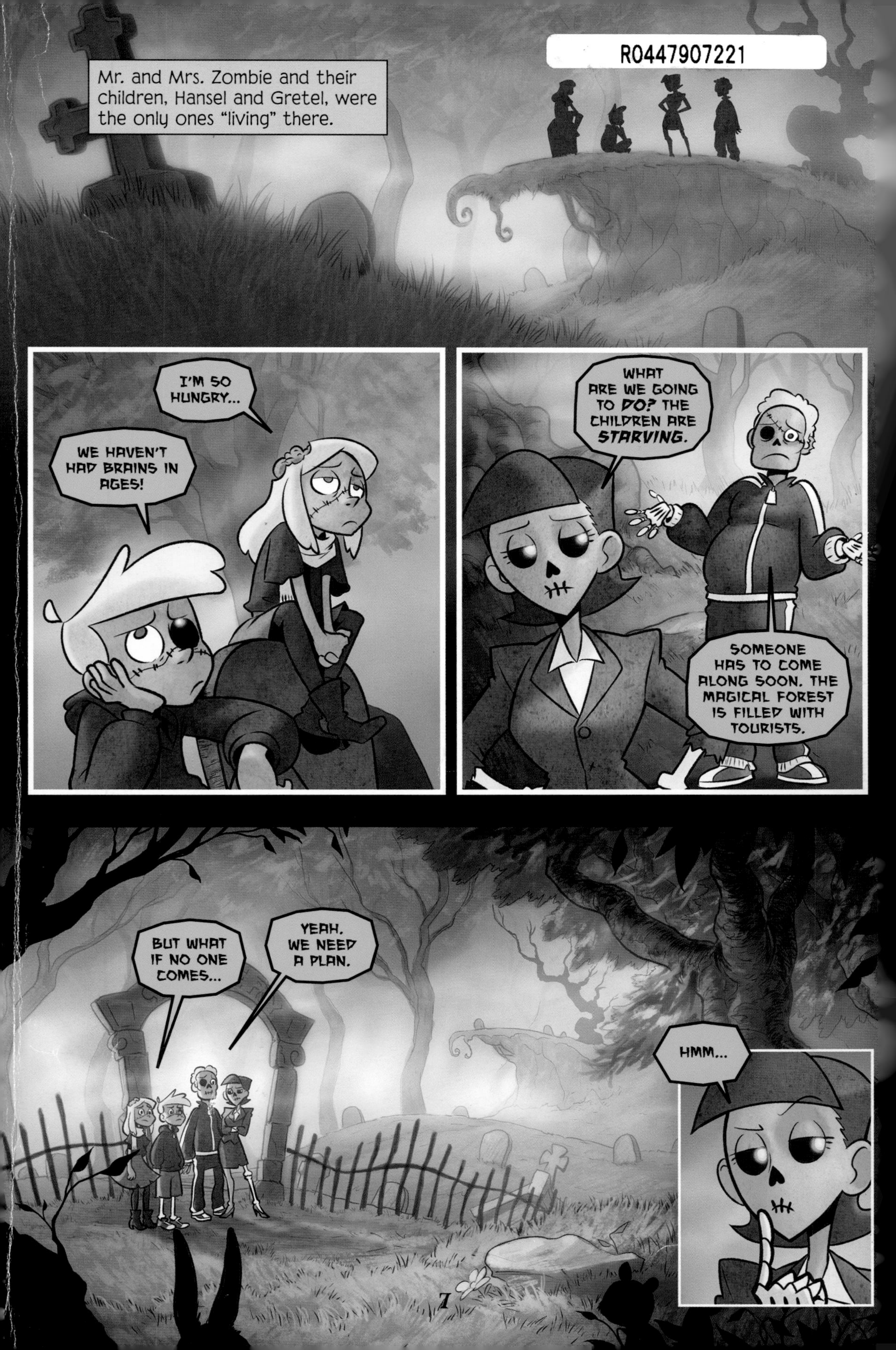
R0447907221
Mr. and Mrs. Zombie and their children, Hansel and Gretel, were the only ones "living" there.
I'M SO HUNGRY...
WE HAVEN'T HAD BRAINS IN AGES!
WHAT ARE WE GOING TO DO? THE CHILDREN ARE STARVING.
SOMEONE HAS TO COME ALONG SOON. THE MAGICAL FOREST IS FILLED WITH TOURISTS.
BUT WHAT IF NO ONE COMES...
YEAH. WE NEED A PLAN.
HMM...

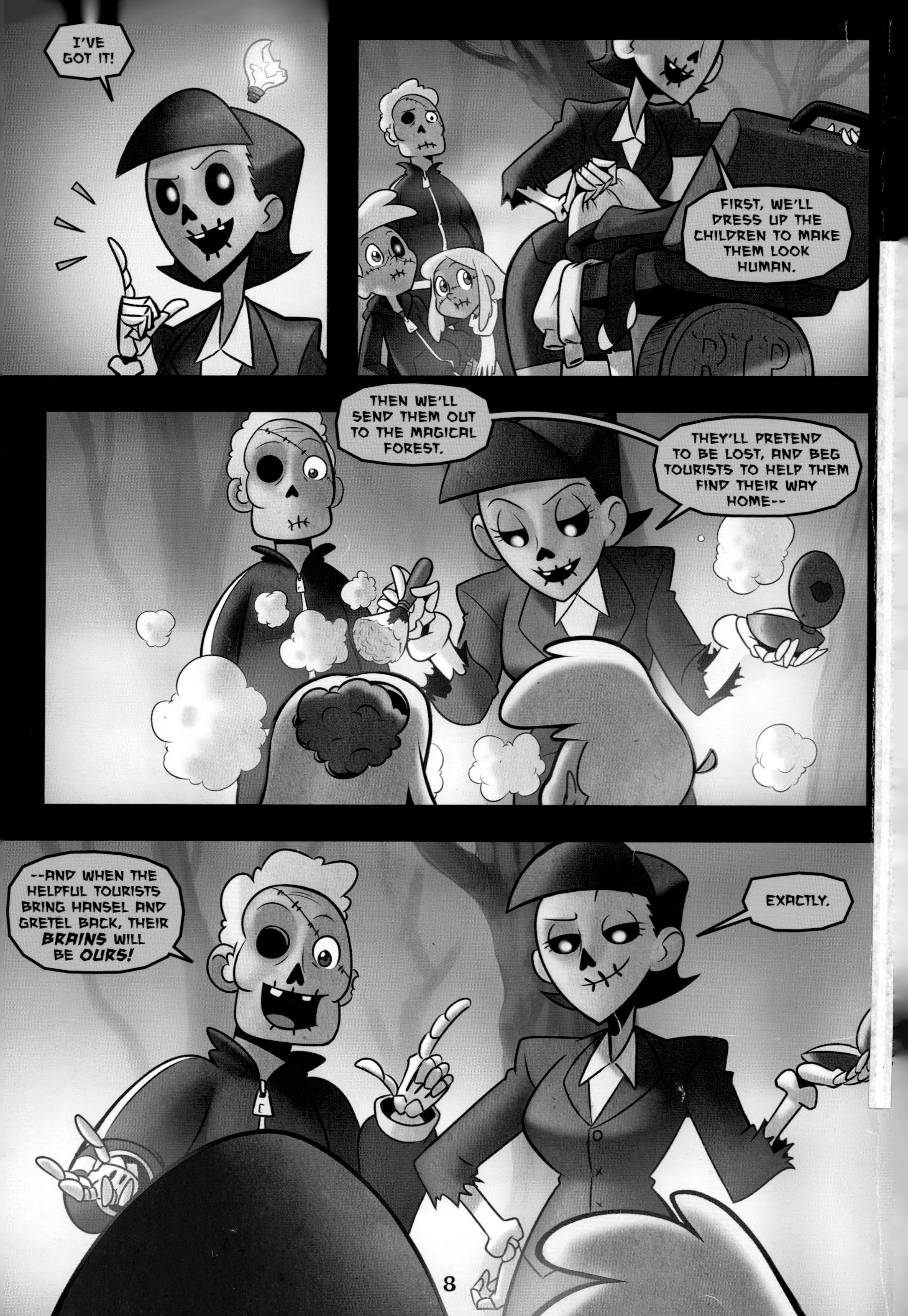
I'VE GOT IT!
FIRST, WE'LL DRESS UP THE CHILDREN TO MAKE THEM LOOK HUMAN.
R.I.P.
THEN WE'LL SEND THEM OUT TO THE MAGICAL FOREST.
THEY'LL PRETEND TO BE LOST, AND BEG TOURISTS TO HELP THEM FIND THEIR WAY HOME--
--AND WHEN THE HELPFUL TOURISTS BRING HANSEL AND GRETEL BACK, THEIR **BRAINS** WILL BE **OURS!**
EXACTLY.

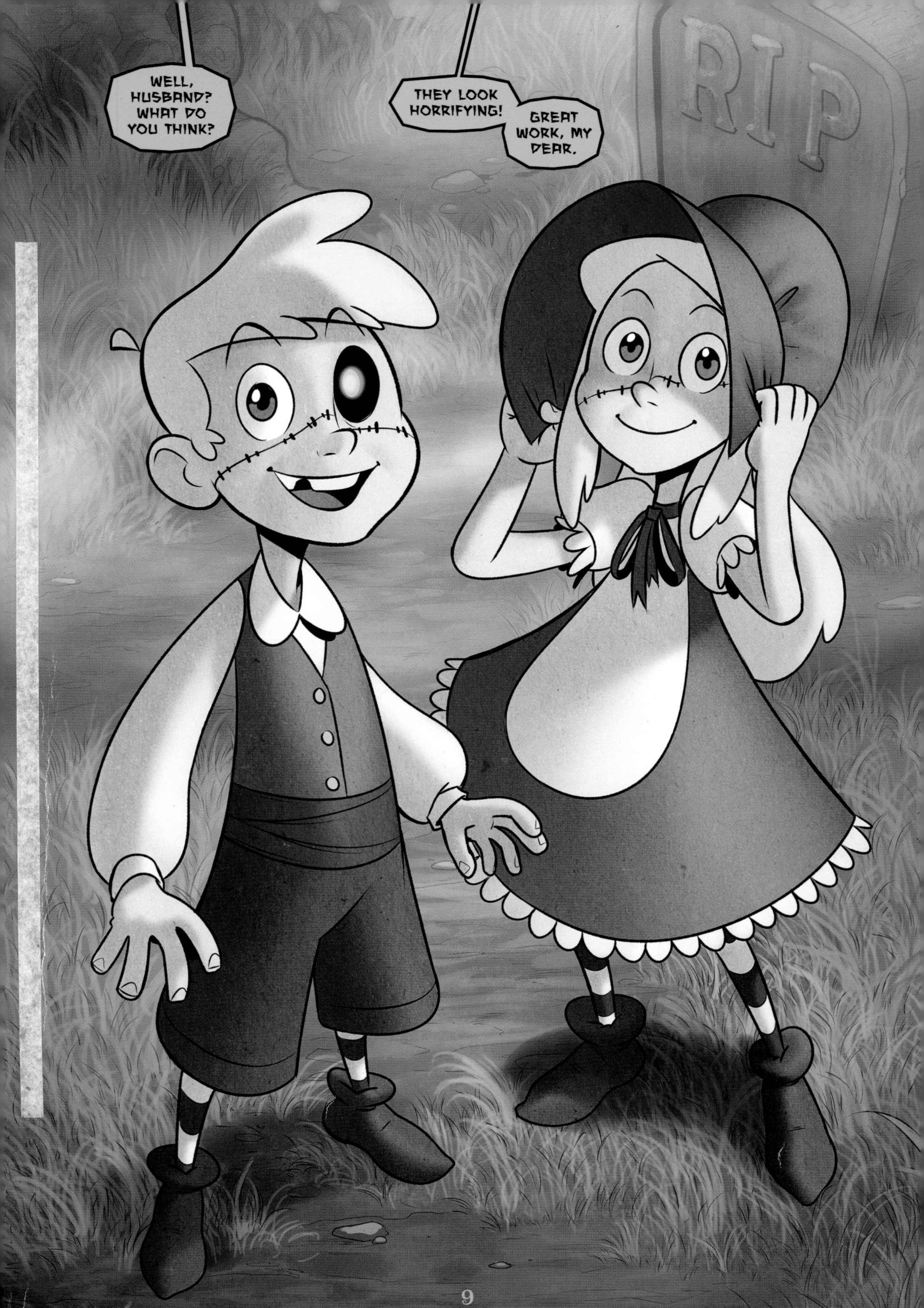
WELL, HUSBAND? WHAT DO YOU THINK?
THEY LOOK HORRIFYING!
GREAT WORK, MY DEAR.
RIP

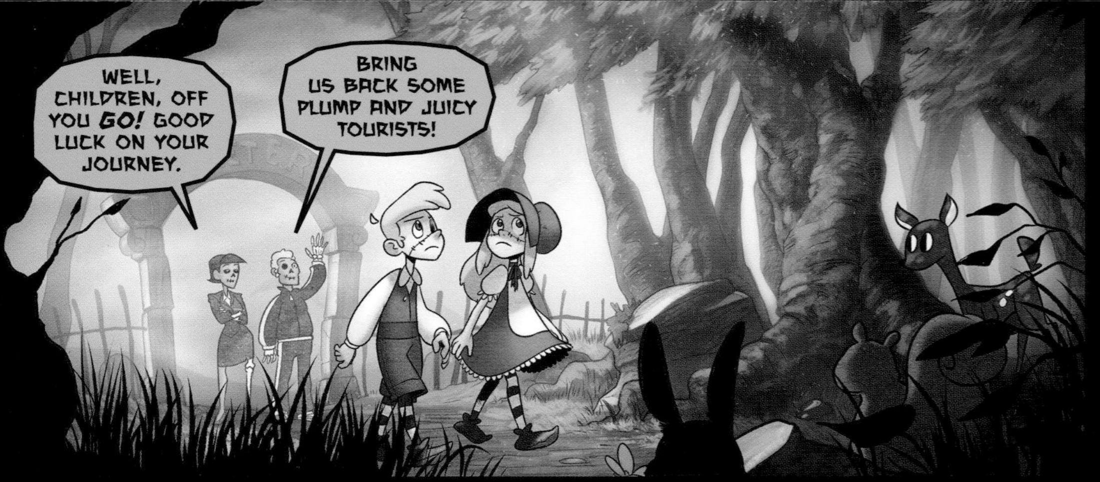
WELL, CHILDREN, OFF YOU *GO!* GOOD LUCK ON YOUR JOURNEY.
BRING US BACK SOME PLUMP AND JUICY TOURISTS!

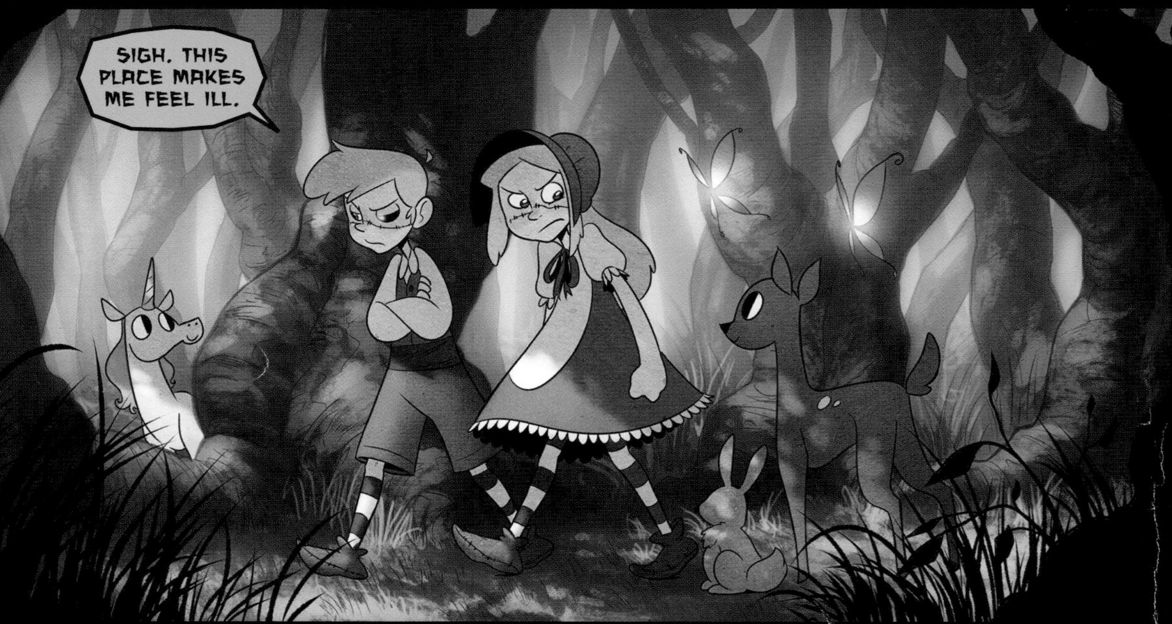
SIGH. THIS PLACE MAKES ME FEEL ILL.

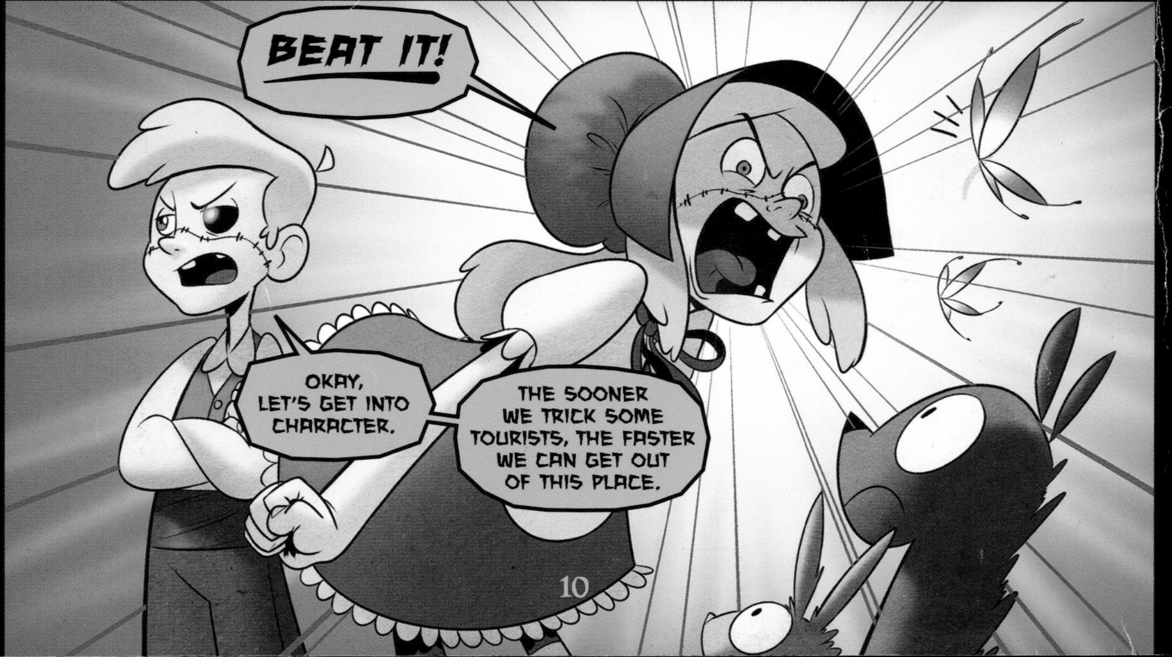
BEAT IT!
OKAY, LET'S GET INTO CHARACTER.
THE SOONER WE TRICK SOME TOURISTS, THE FASTER WE CAN GET OUT OF THIS PLACE.

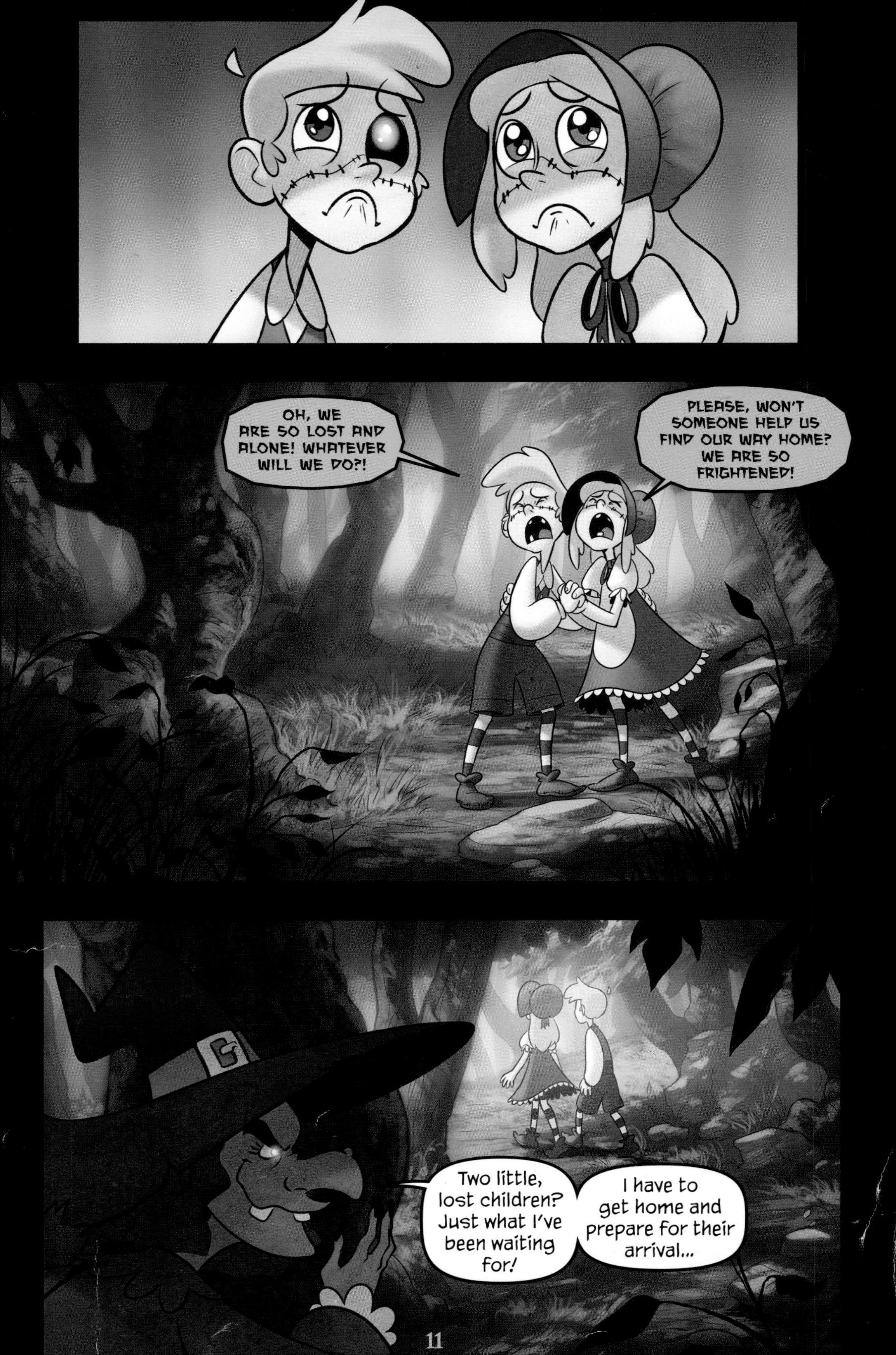
OH, WE ARE SO LOST AND ALONE! WHATEVER WILL WE DO?!
PLEASE, WON'T SOMEONE HELP US FIND OUR WAY HOME? WE ARE SO FRIGHTENED!
Two little, lost children? Just what I've been waiting for!
I have to get home and prepare for their arrival...

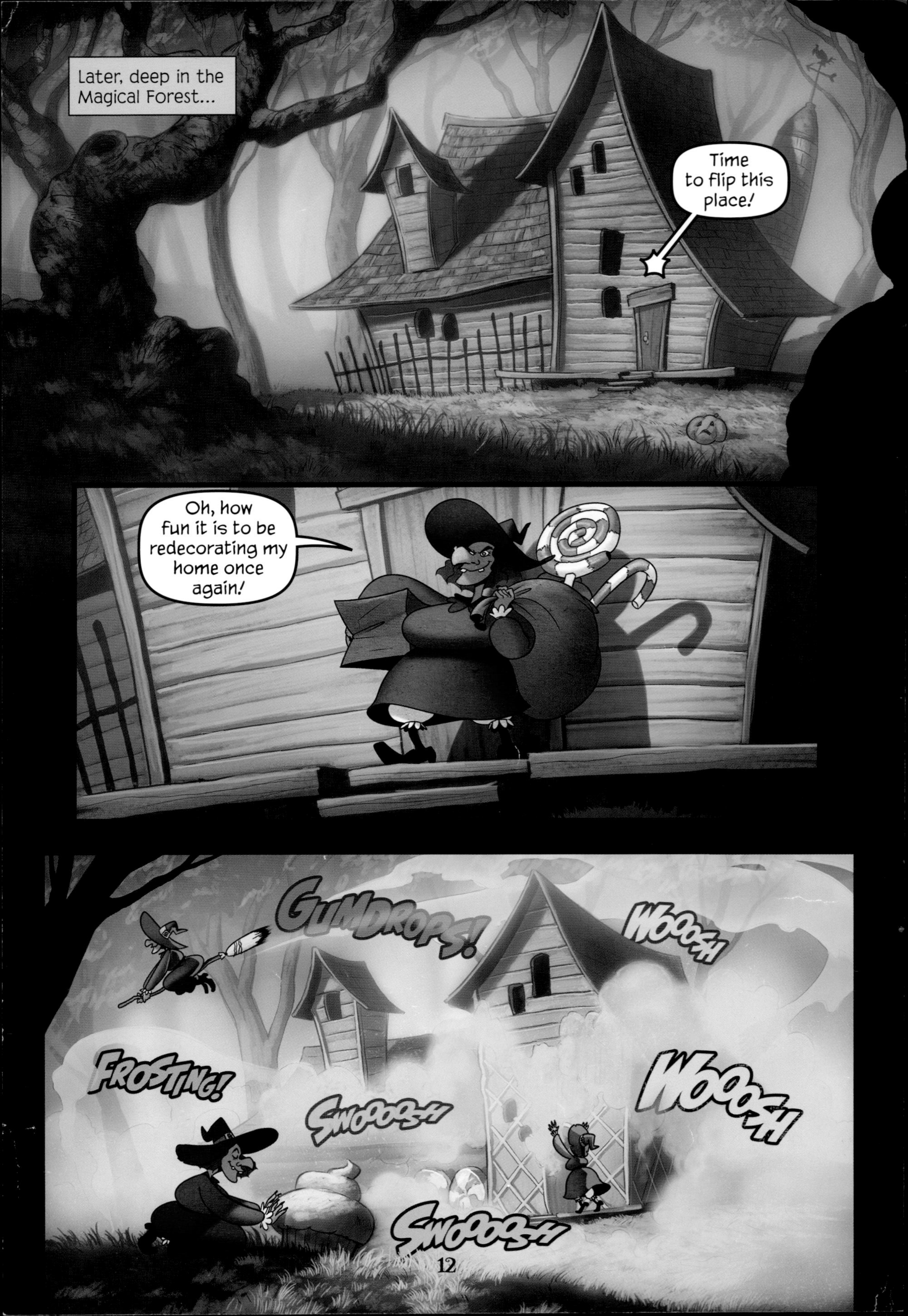
Later, deep in the Magical Forest...
Time to flip this place!
Oh, how fun it is to be redecorating my home once again!
GUMDROPS!
WOOOSH
FROSTING!
SWOOOSH
WOOOSH
SWOOOSH

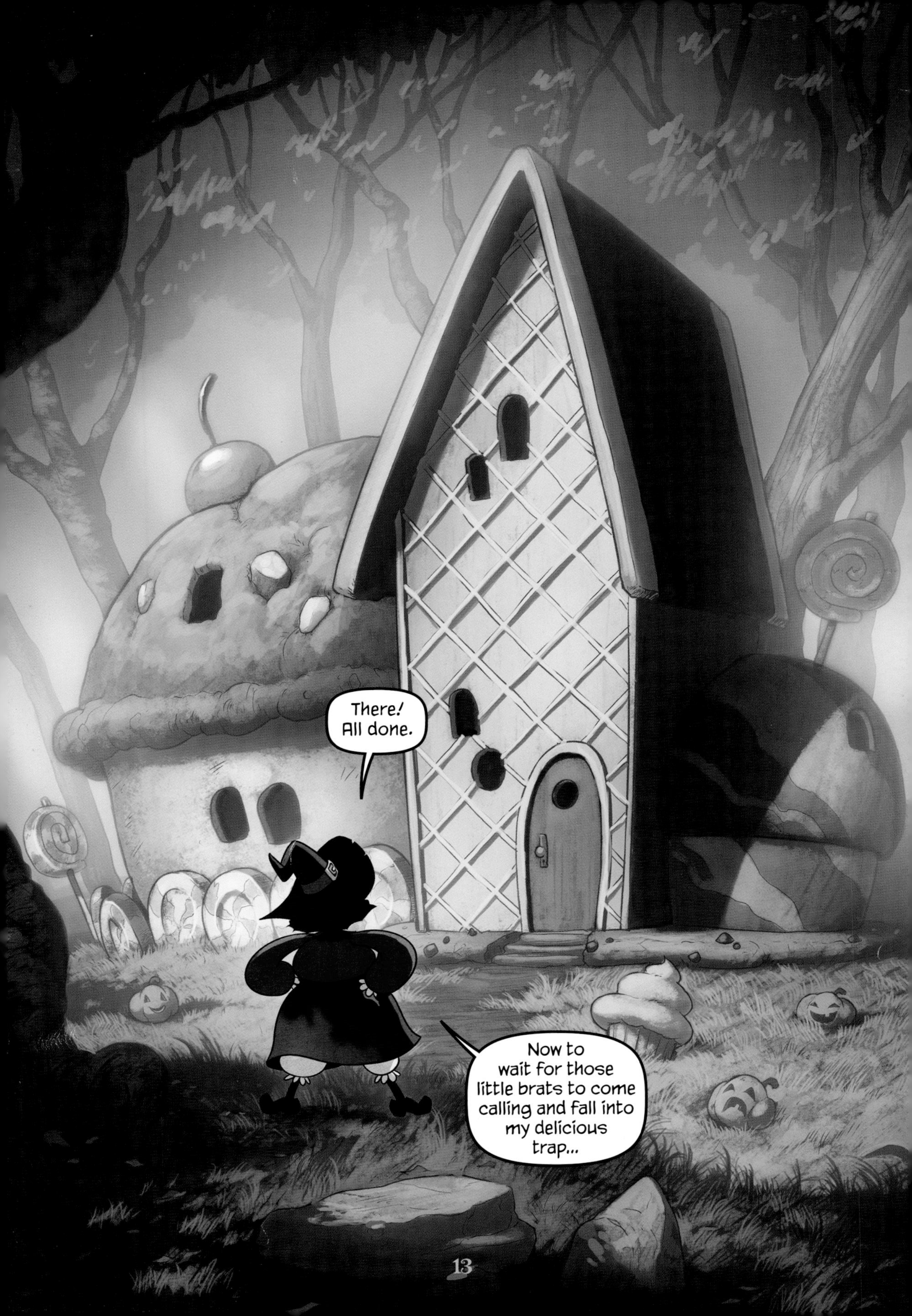
There! All done.
Now to wait for those little brats to come calling and fall into my delicious trap...

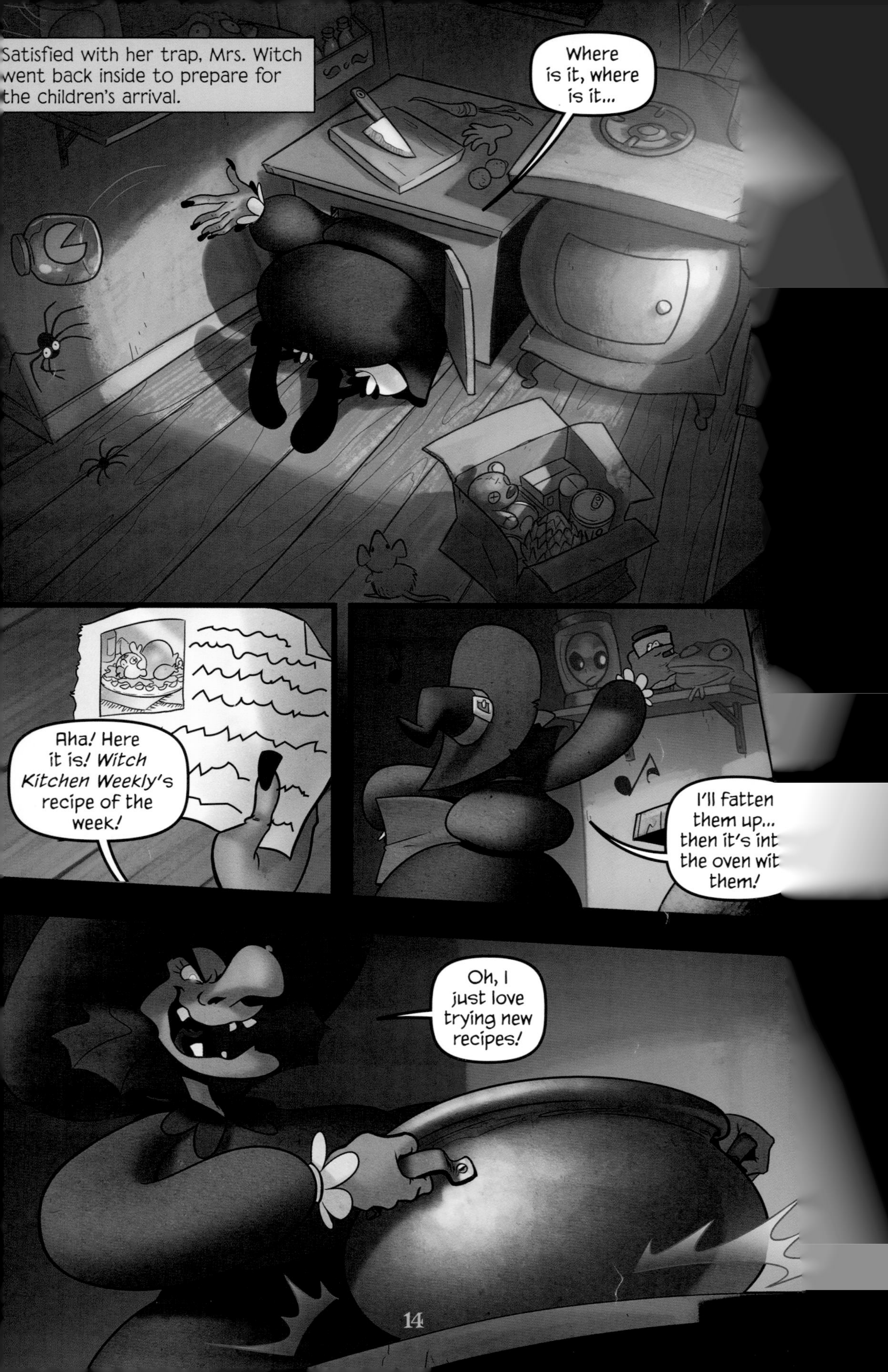

Satisfied with her trap, Mrs. Witch went back inside to prepare for the children's arrival.
Where is it, where is it...
Aha! Here it is! *Witch Kitchen Weekly*'s recipe of the week!
I'll fatten them up... then it's int the oven wit them!
Oh, I just love trying new recipes!

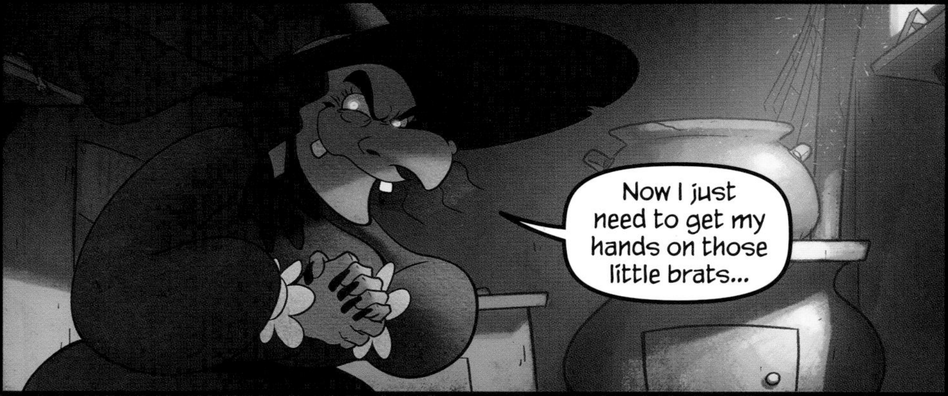
Now I just need to get my hands on those little brats...

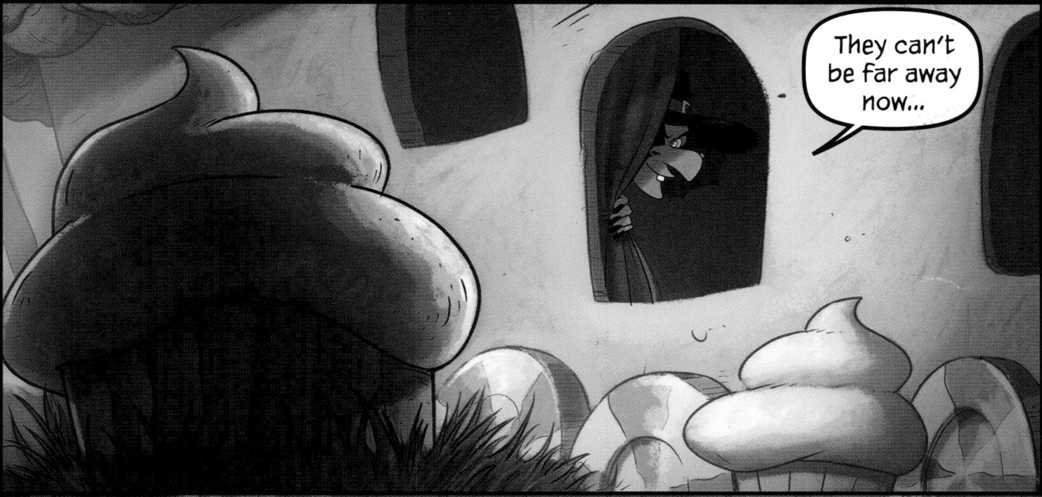
They can't be far away now...

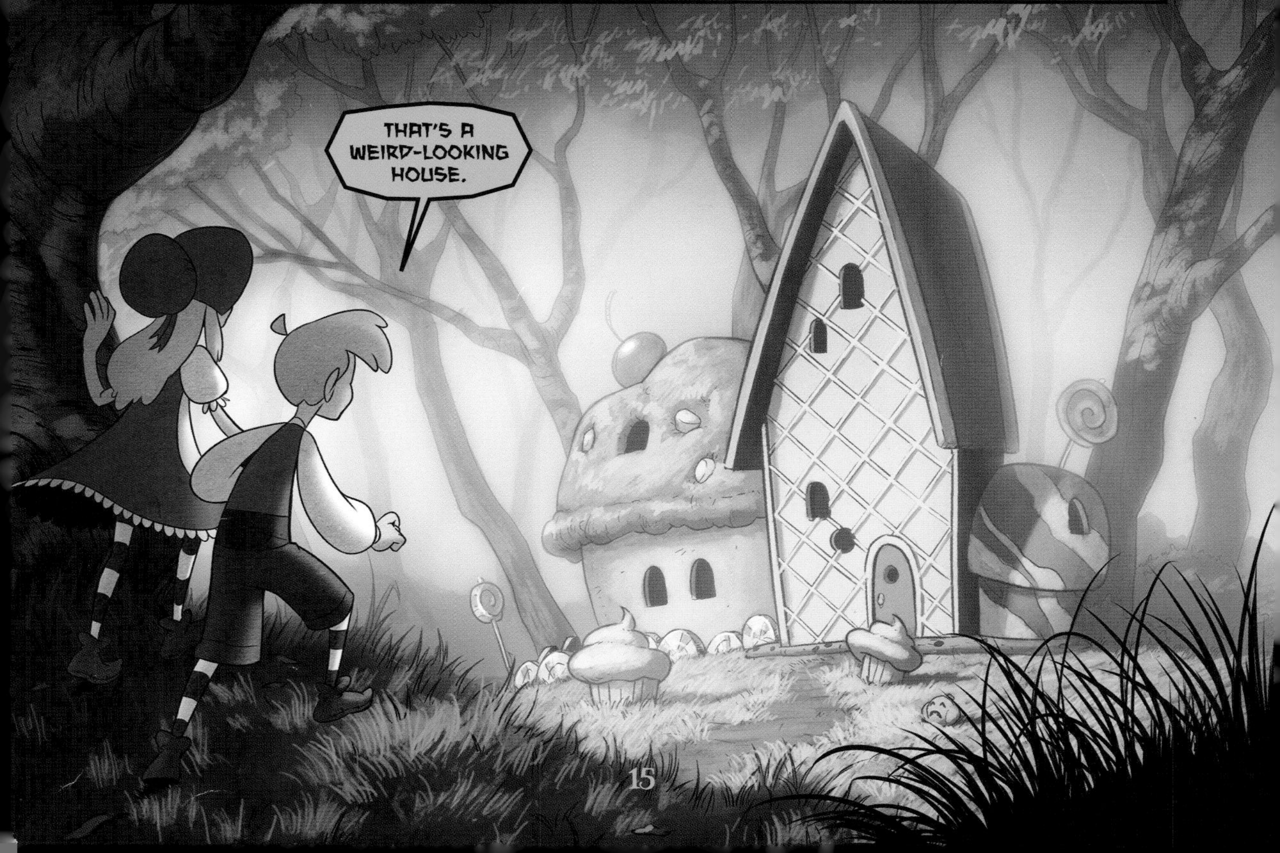
THAT'S A WEIRD-LOOKING HOUSE.

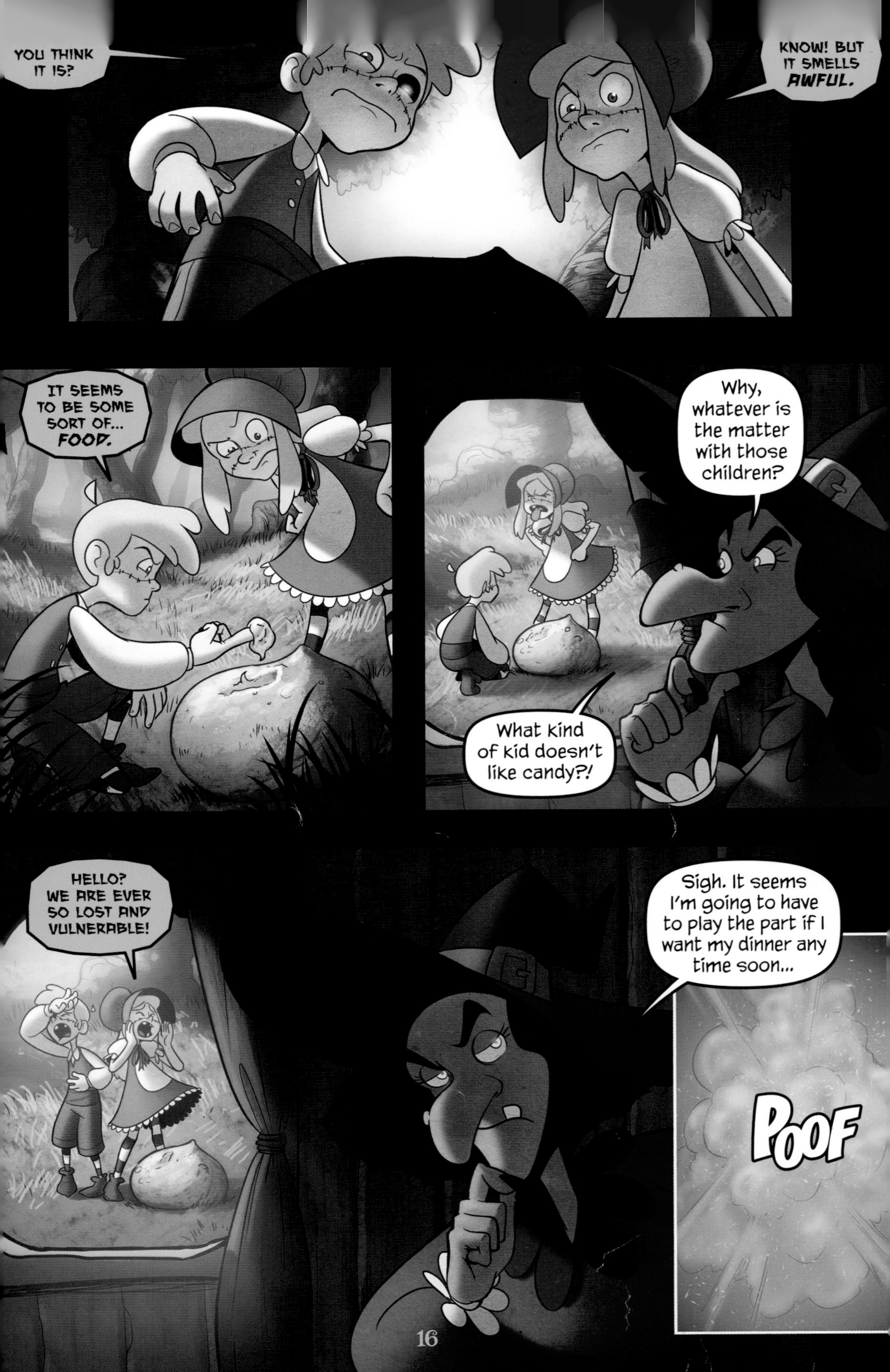

YOU THINK IT IS?
KNOW! BUT IT SMELLS AWFUL.
IT SEEMS TO BE SOME SORT OF... FOOD.
Why, whatever is the matter with those children?
What kind of kid doesn't like candy?!
HELLO? WE ARE EVER SO LOST AND VULNERABLE!
Sigh. It seems I'm going to have to play the part if I want my dinner any time soon...
POOF

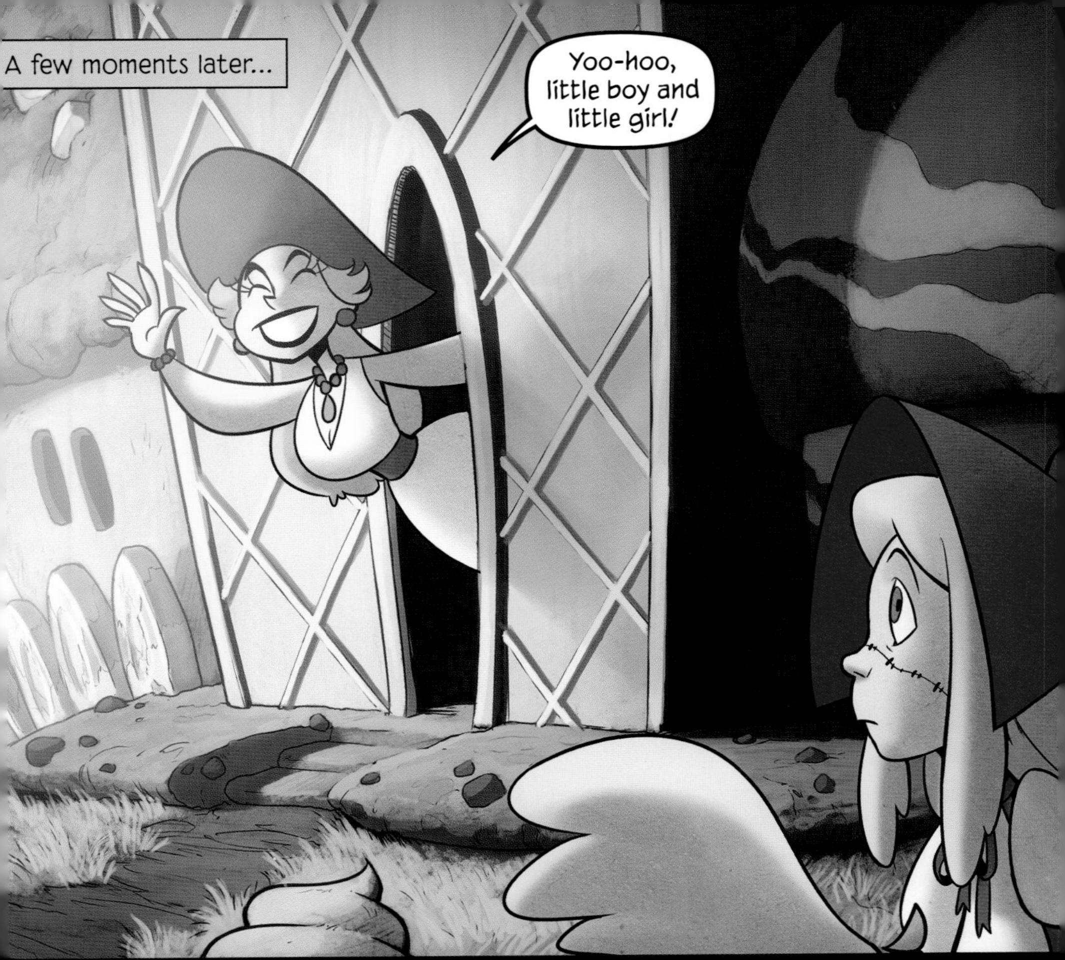
A few moments later...
Yoo-hoo, little boy and little girl!

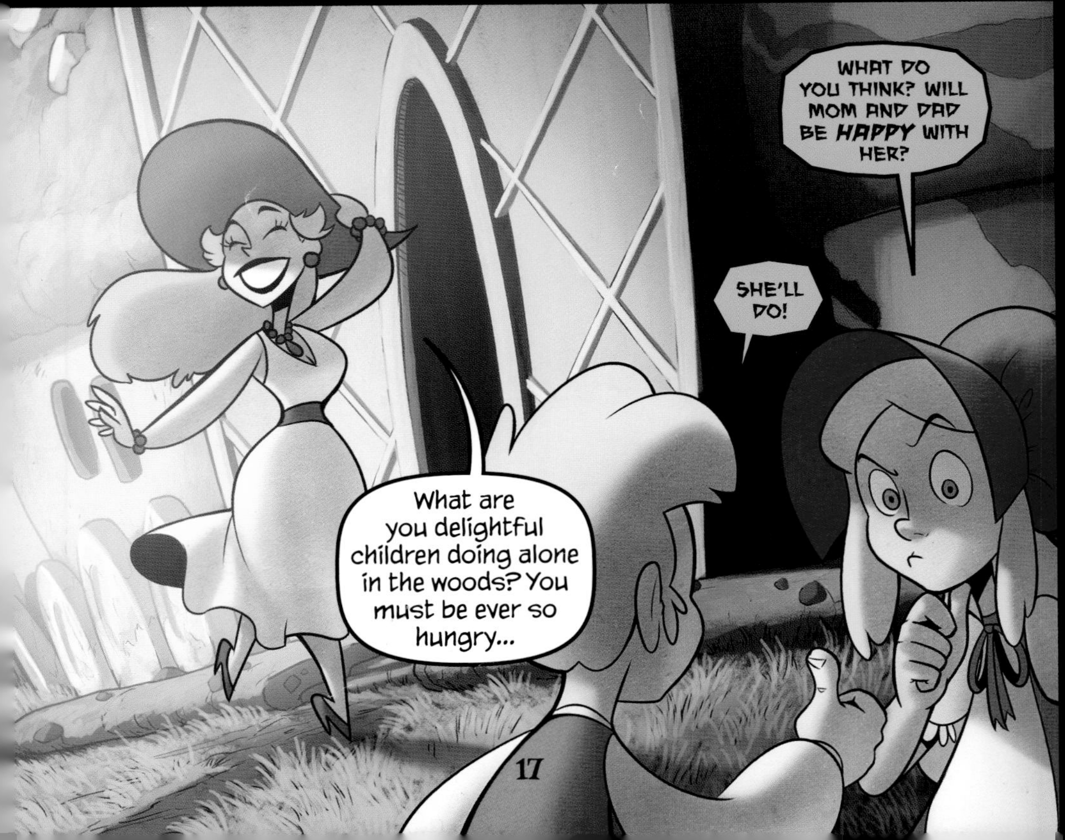
WHAT DO YOU THINK? WILL MOM AND DAD BE HAPPY WITH HER?
SHE'LL DO!
What are you delightful children doing alone in the woods? You must be ever so hungry...

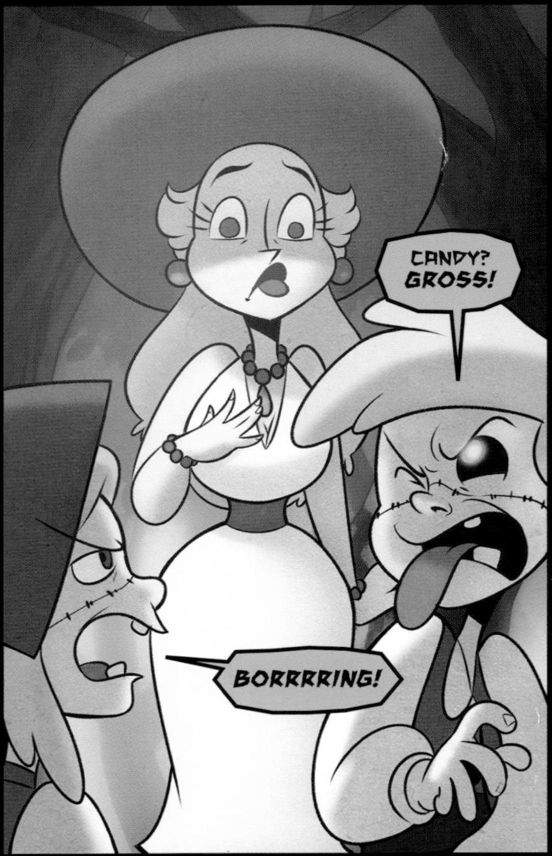
CANDY? GROSS!
BORRRRING!

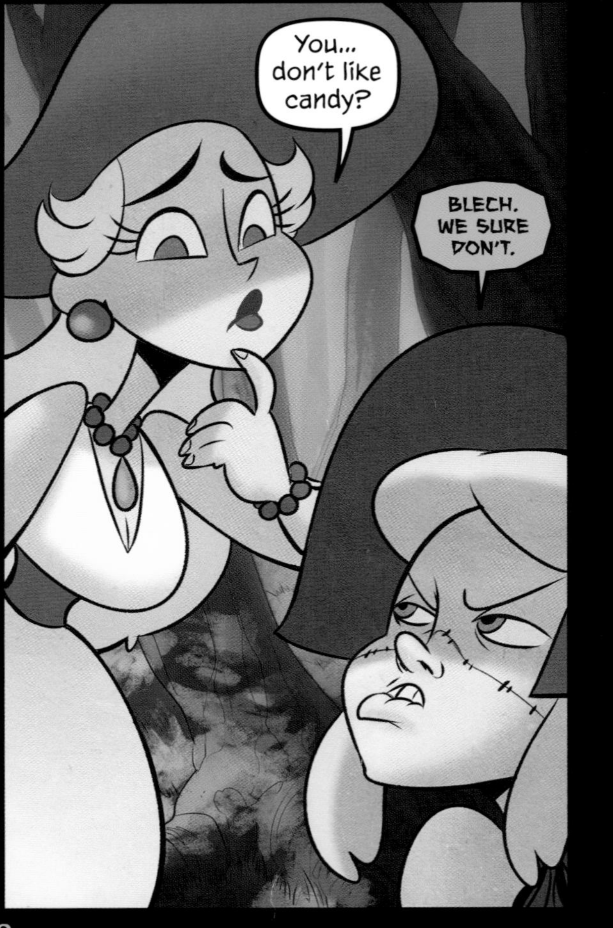
You... don't like candy?
BLECH. WE SURE DON'T.

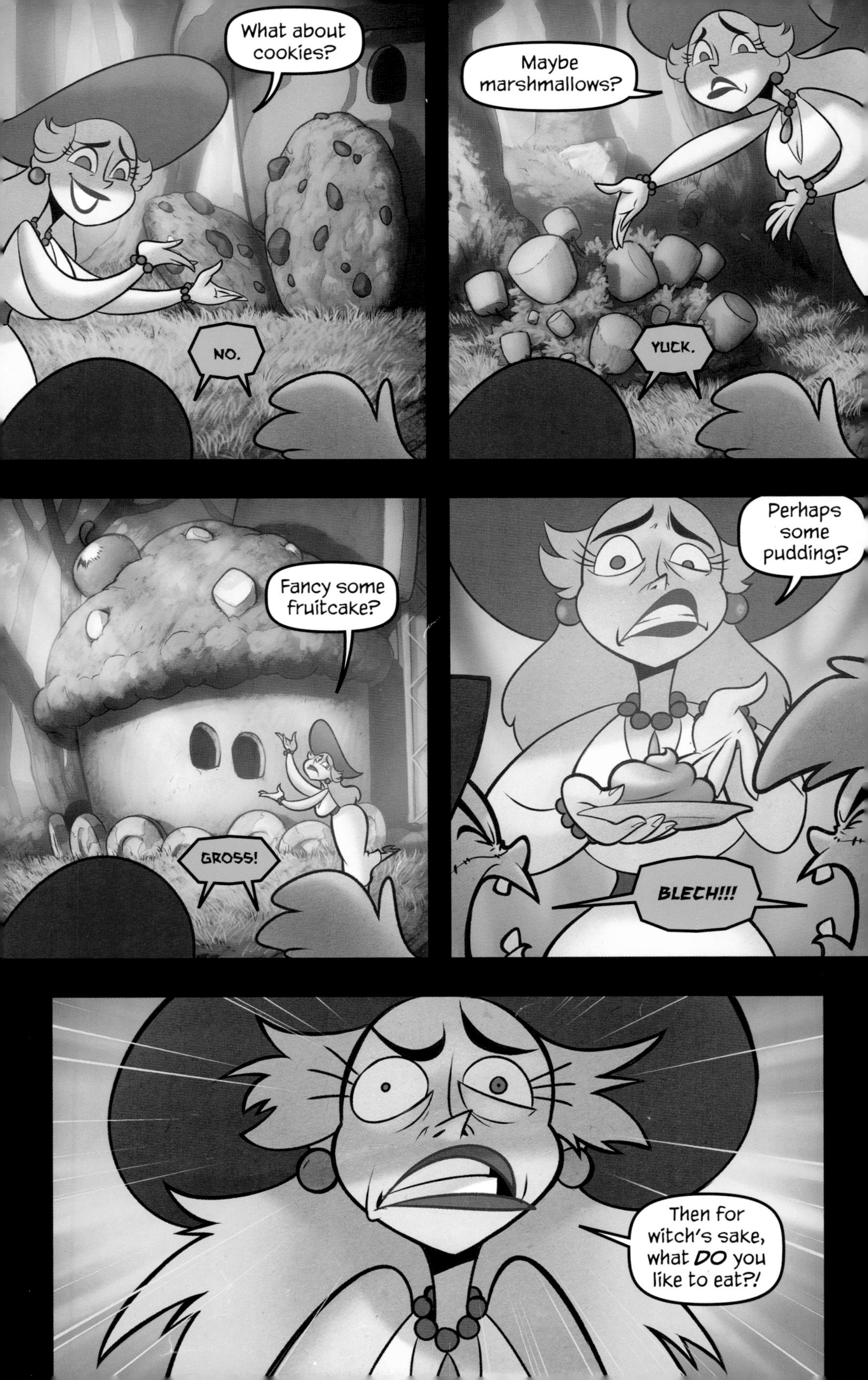
What about cookies?
NO.
Maybe marshmallows?
YUCK.
Fancy some fruitcake?
GROSS!
Perhaps some pudding?
BLECH!!!
Then for witch's sake, what *DO* you like to eat?!

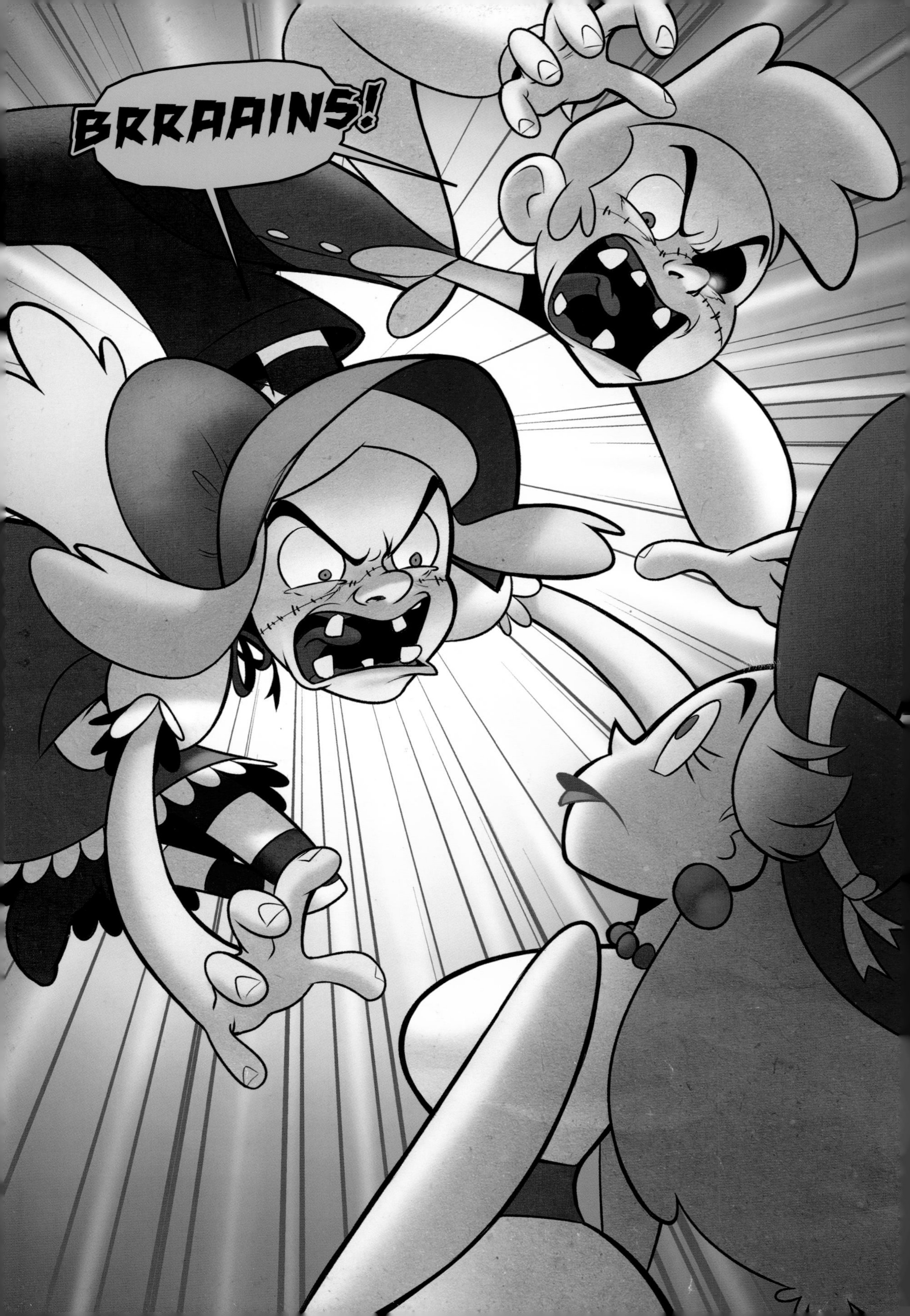
BRRAAINS!

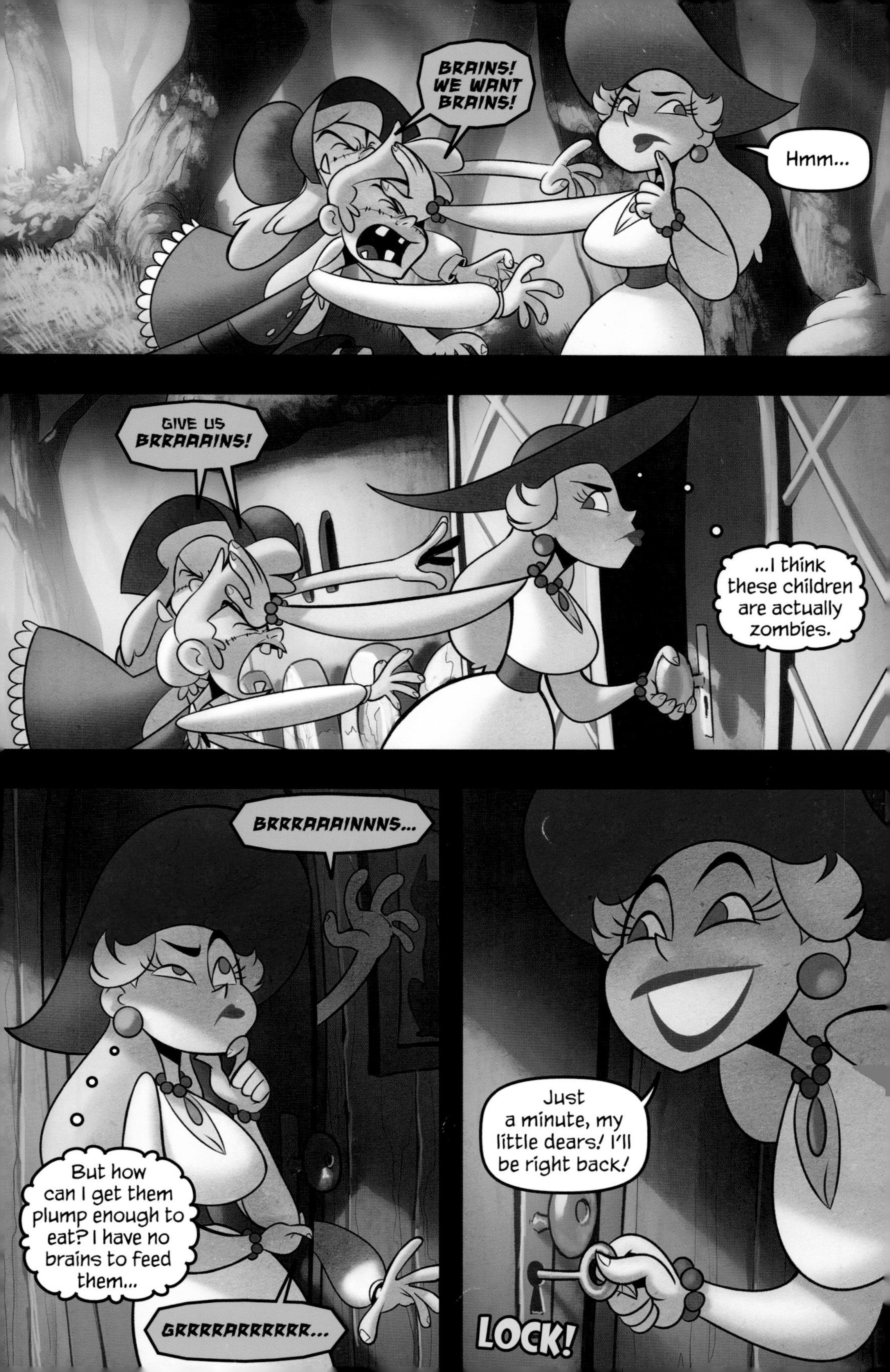
BRAINS! WE WANT BRAINS!
Hmm...
GIVE US BRRAAAINS!
...I think these children are actually zombies.
BRRRAAAINNNS...
But how can I get them plump enough to eat? I have no brains to feed them...
GRRRRARRRRRR...
Just a minute, my little dears! I'll be right back!
LOCK!

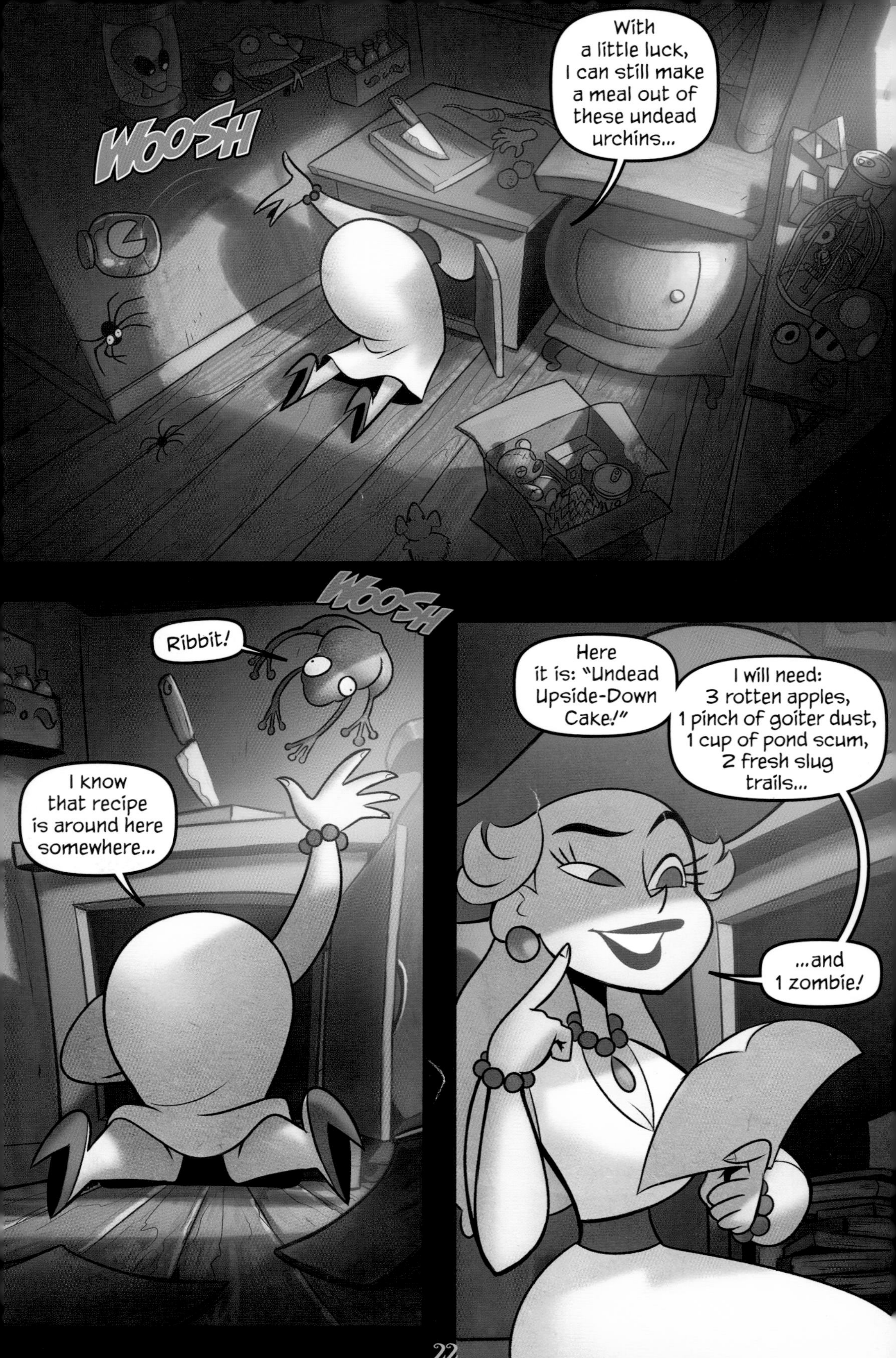
WOOSH
With a little luck, I can still make a meal out of these undead urchins...
WOOSH
Ribbit!
I know that recipe is around here somewhere...
Here it is: "Undead Upside-Down Cake!"
I will need: 3 rotten apples, 1 pinch of goiter dust, 1 cup of pond scum, 2 fresh slug trails...
...and 1 zombie!

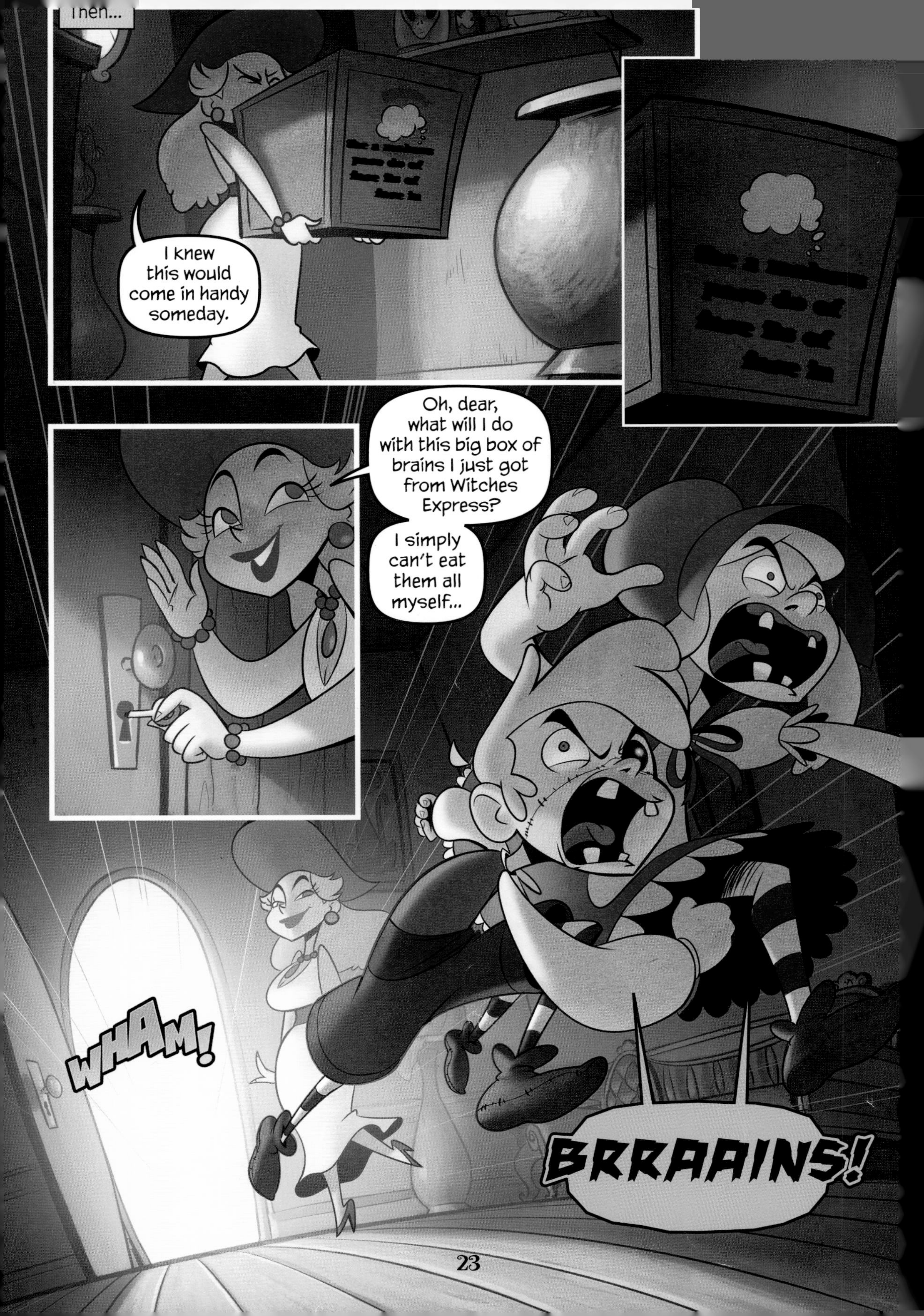
Then...
I knew this would come in handy someday.
Oh, dear, what will I do with this big box of brains I just got from Witches Express?
I simply can't eat them all myself...
WHAM!
BRRAAINS!

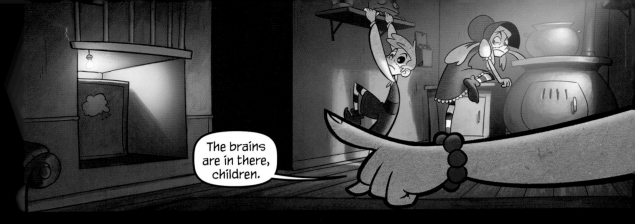

The brains are in there, children.

ME FIRST! BRAINS!!

NO-- ME FIRST! MINE!!

Manners, please! One at a time.

NO FAIR! HE ALWAYS GETS TO EAT FIRST.

≶GULP!≷

SLAM

HEY, LET ME OUT OF HERE!

Hee-hee-hee! You're all mine now, boy!

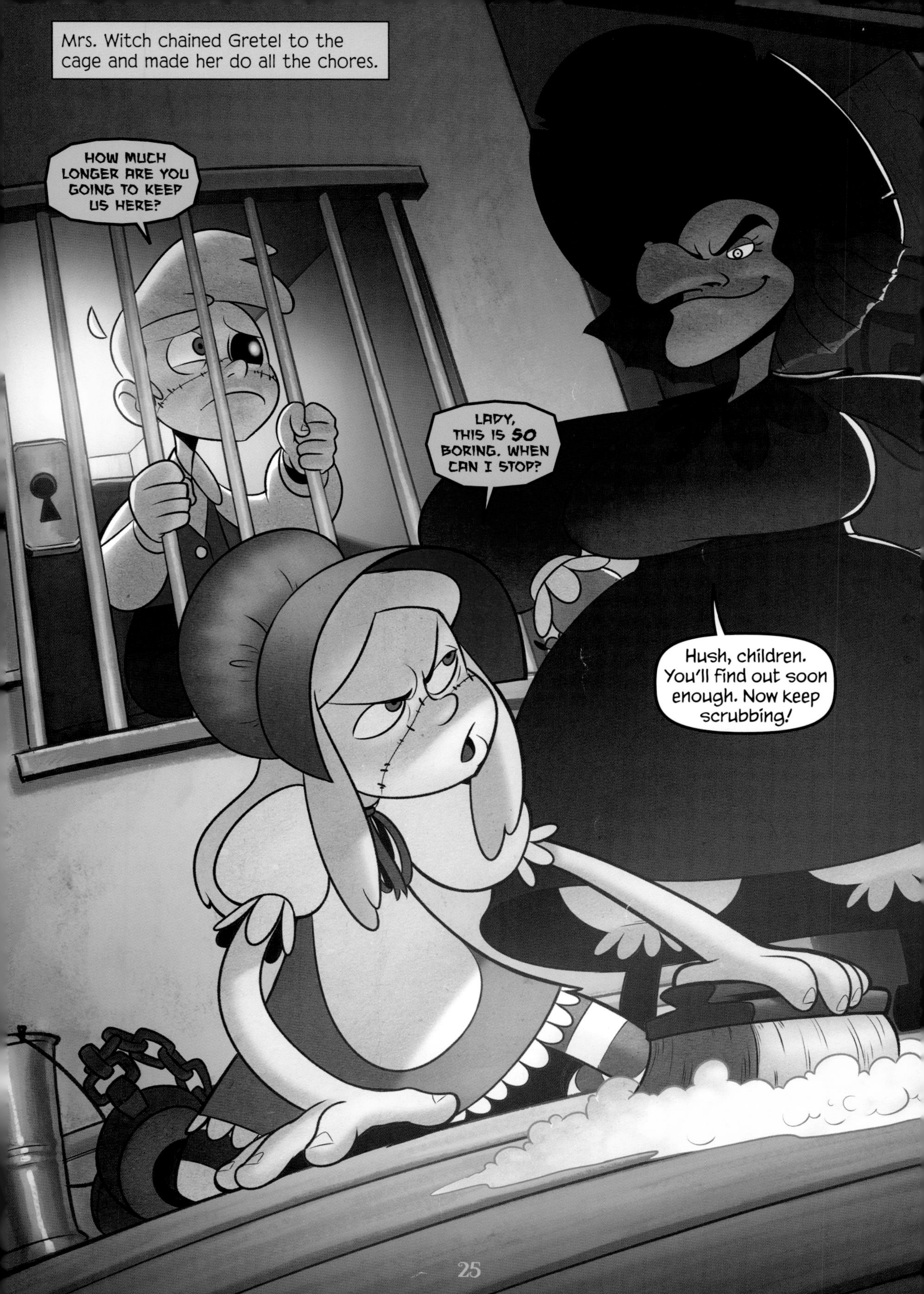
Mrs. Witch chained Gretel to the cage and made her do all the chores.
HOW MUCH LONGER ARE YOU GOING TO KEEP US HERE?
LADY, THIS IS SO BORING. WHEN CAN I STOP?
Hush, children. You'll find out soon enough. Now keep scrubbing!

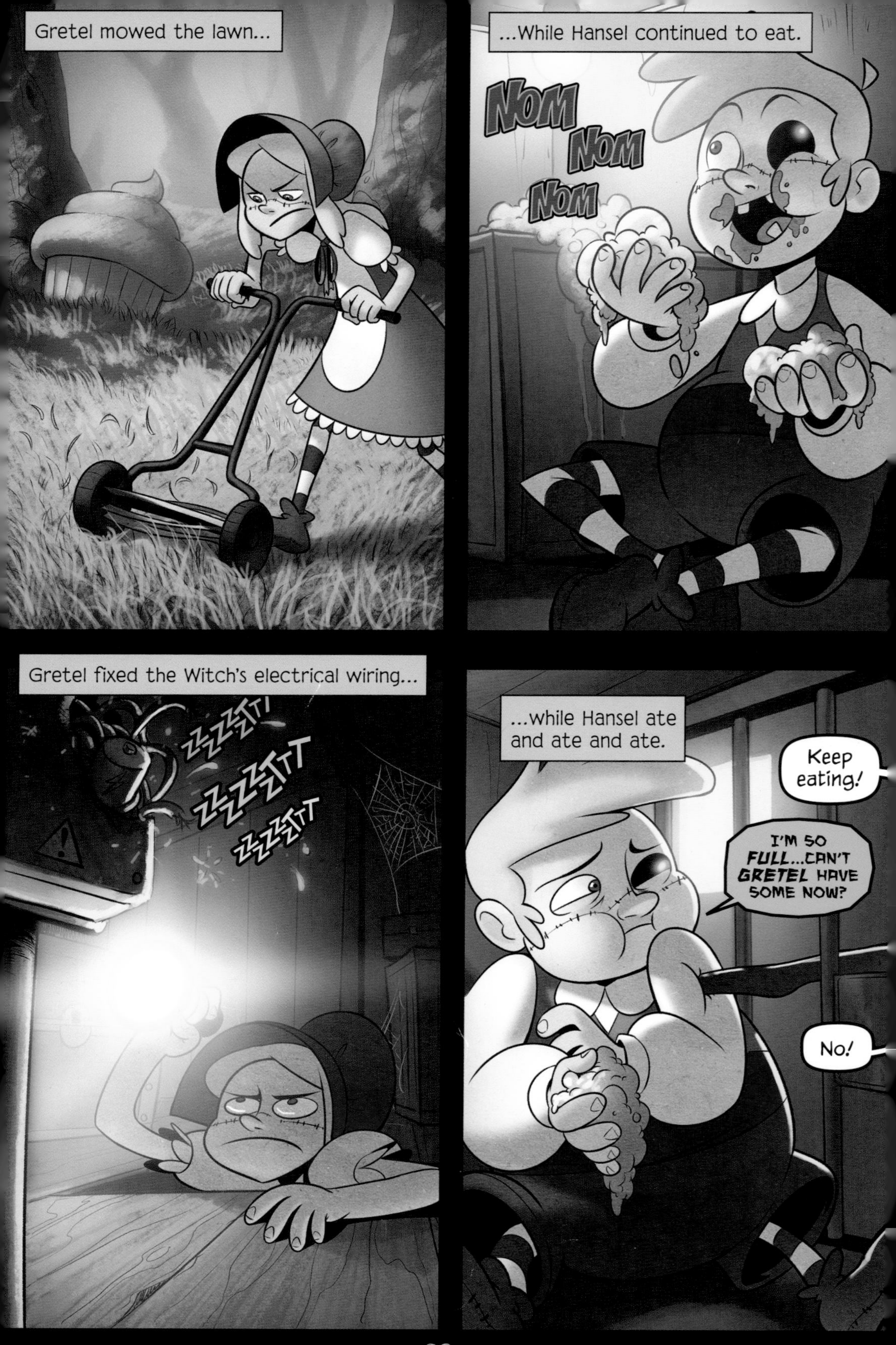
Gretel mowed the lawn...
...While Hansel continued to eat.
NOM
NOM
NOM
Gretel fixed the Witch's electrical wiring...
ZZZZZT!
ZZZZZTTT
ZZZZZTTT
...while Hansel ate and ate and ate.
Keep eating!
I'M SO FULL...CAN'T GRETEL HAVE SOME NOW?
No!

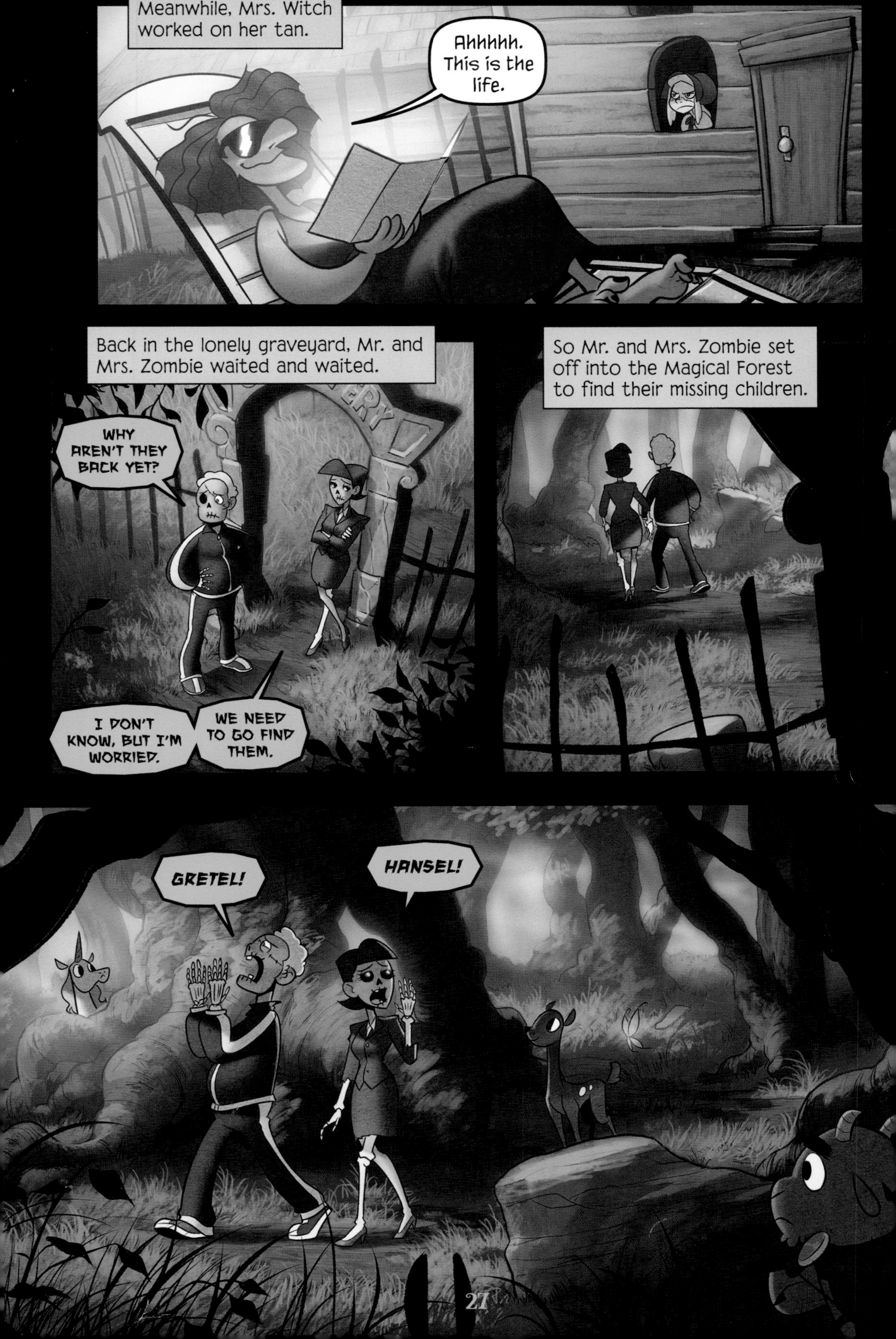
Meanwhile, Mrs. Witch worked on her tan.
Ahhhhh. This is the life.
Back in the lonely graveyard, Mr. and Mrs. Zombie waited and waited.
WHY AREN'T THEY BACK YET?
I DON'T KNOW, BUT I'M WORRIED.
WE NEED TO GO FIND THEM.
So Mr. and Mrs. Zombie set off into the Magical Forest to find their missing children.
GRETEL!
HANSEL!

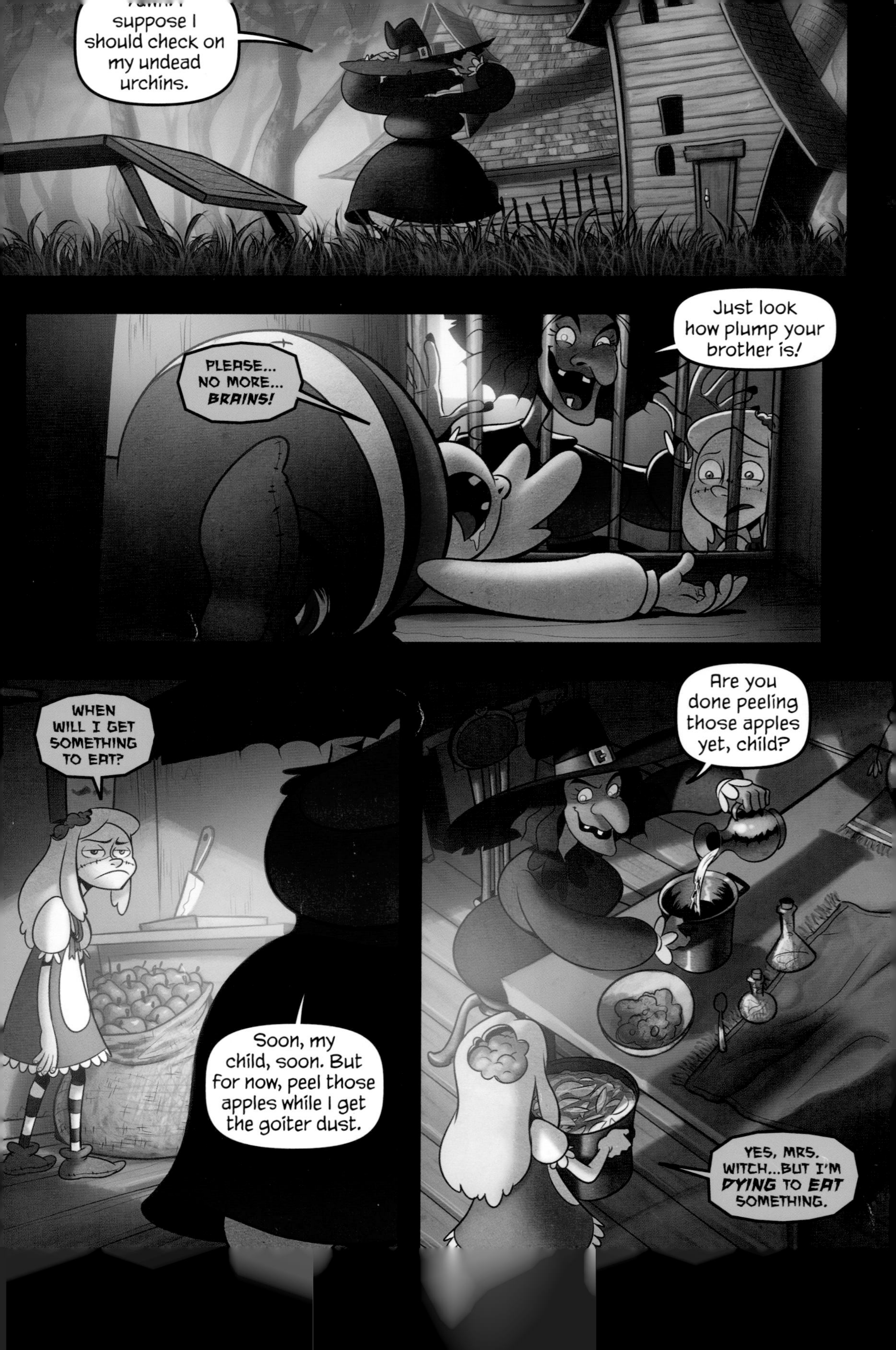
suppose I should check on my undead urchins.
PLEASE... NO MORE... BRAINS!
Just look how plump your brother is!
WHEN WILL I GET SOMETHING TO EAT?
Soon, my child, soon. But for now, peel those apples while I get the goiter dust.
Are you done peeling those apples yet, child?
YES, MRS. WITCH...BUT I'M DYING TO EAT SOMETHING.

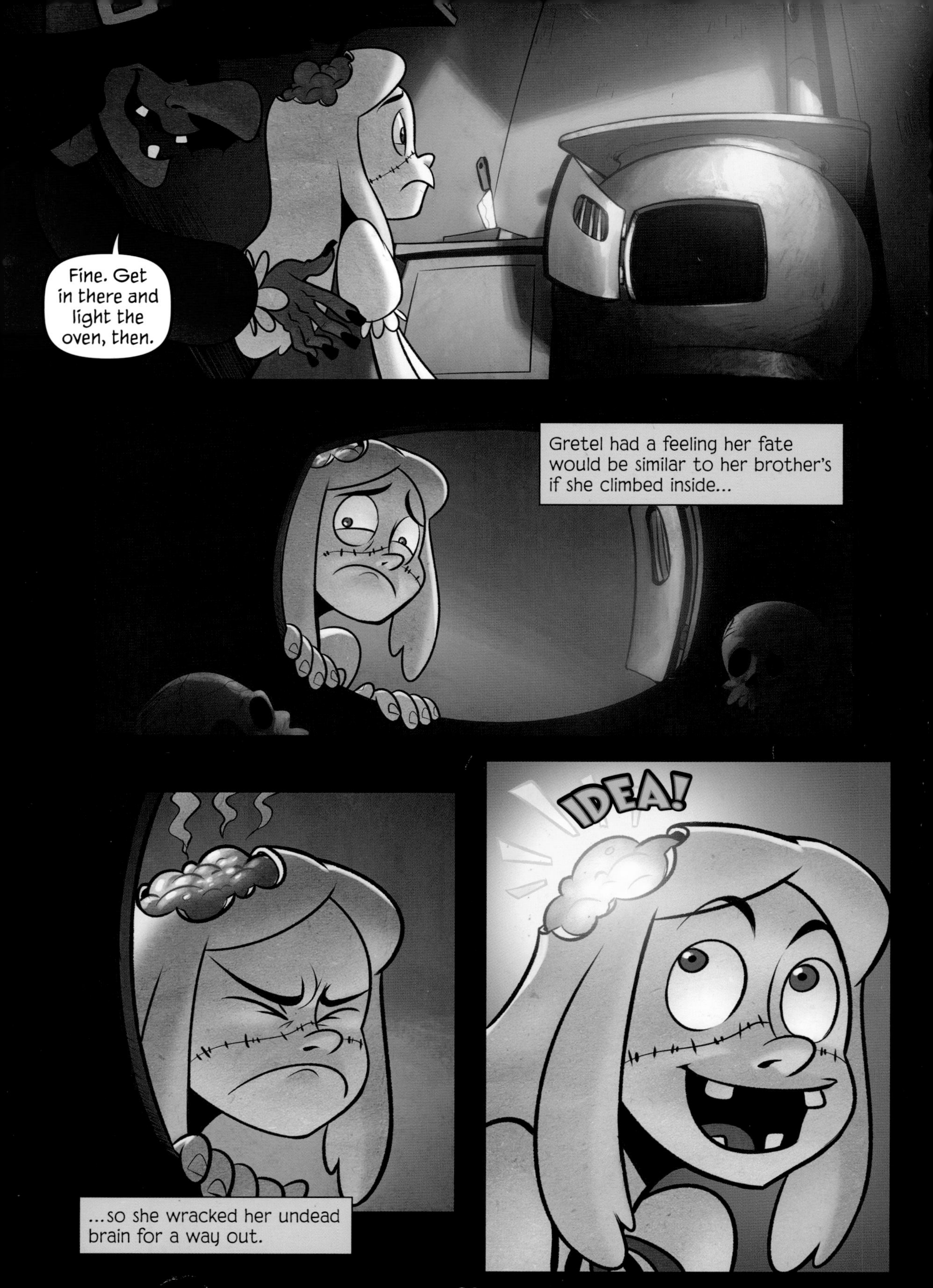
Fine. Get in there and light the oven, then.
Gretel had a feeling her fate would be similar to her brother's if she climbed inside...
...so she wracked her undead brain for a way out.
IDEA!

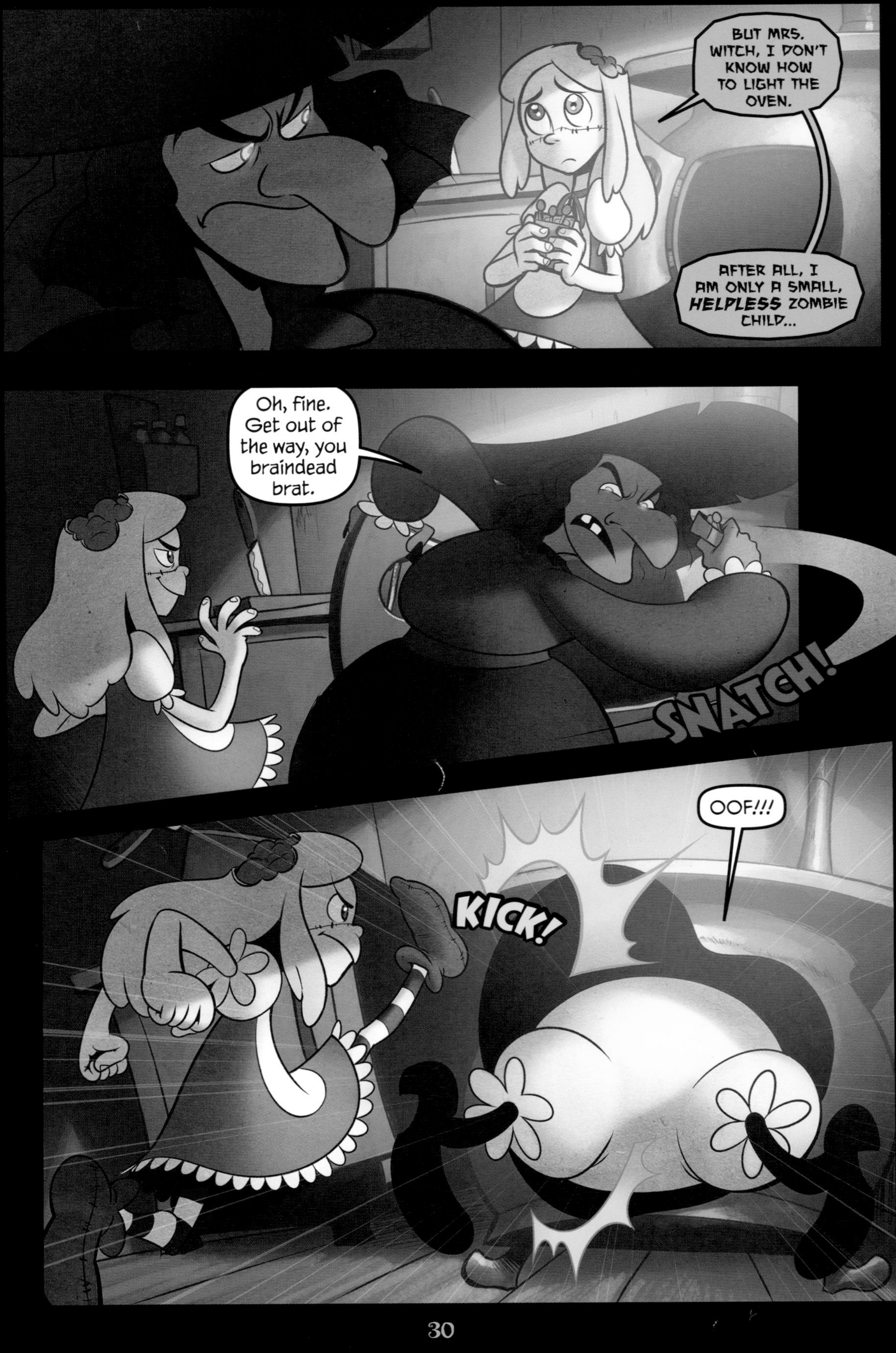
BUT MRS. WITCH, I DON'T KNOW HOW TO LIGHT THE OVEN.
AFTER ALL, I AM ONLY A SMALL, **HELPLESS** ZOMBIE CHILD...
Oh, fine. Get out of the way, you braindead brat.
SNATCH!
KICK!
OOF!!!

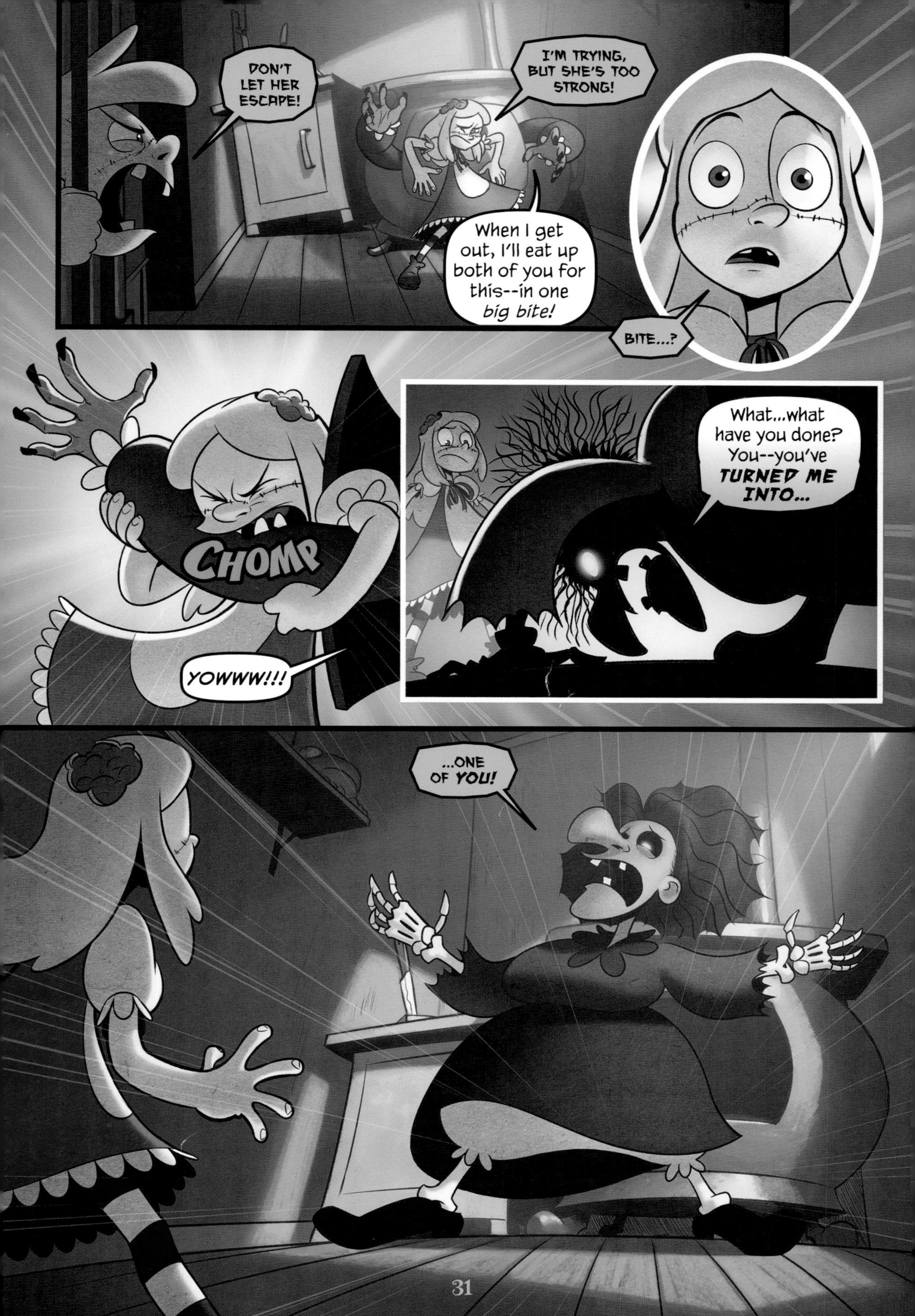
DON'T LET HER ESCAPE!
I'M TRYING, BUT SHE'S TOO STRONG!
When I get out, I'll eat up both of you for this--in one *big bite!*
BITE...?
CHOMP
YOWWW!!!
What...what have you done? You--you've **TURNED ME INTO...**
...ONE OF **YOU!**

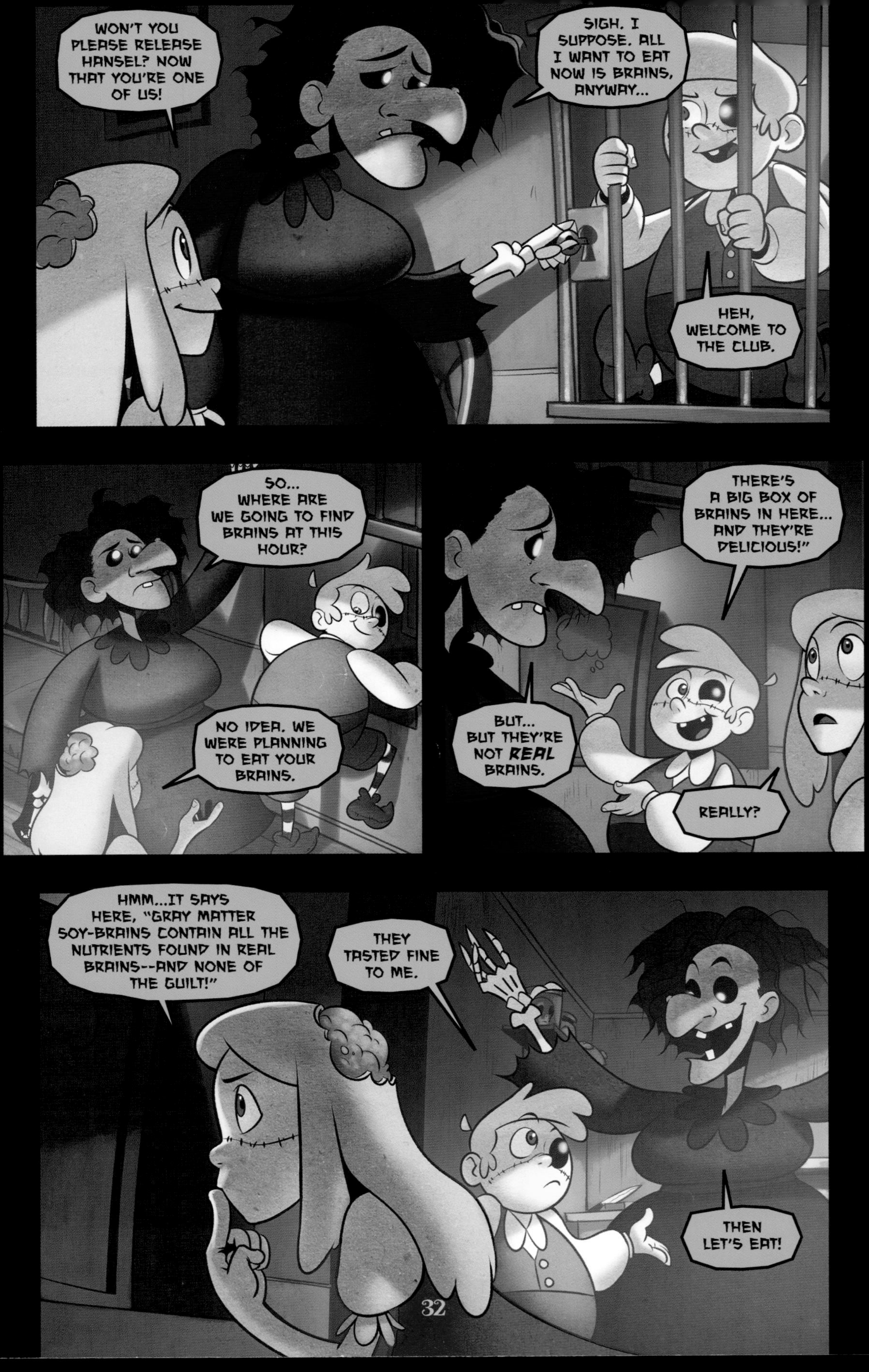

WON'T YOU PLEASE RELEASE HANSEL? NOW THAT YOU'RE ONE OF US!
SIGH. I SUPPOSE. ALL I WANT TO EAT NOW IS BRAINS, ANYWAY...
HEH, WELCOME TO THE CLUB.
SO... WHERE ARE WE GOING TO FIND BRAINS AT THIS HOUR?
NO IDEA. WE WERE PLANNING TO EAT YOUR BRAINS.
THERE'S A BIG BOX OF BRAINS IN HERE... AND THEY'RE DELICIOUS!"
BUT... BUT THEY'RE NOT REAL BRAINS.
REALLY?
HMM...IT SAYS HERE, "GRAY MATTER SOY-BRAINS CONTAIN ALL THE NUTRIENTS FOUND IN REAL BRAINS--AND NONE OF THE GUILT!"
THEY TASTED FINE TO ME.
THEN LET'S EAT!

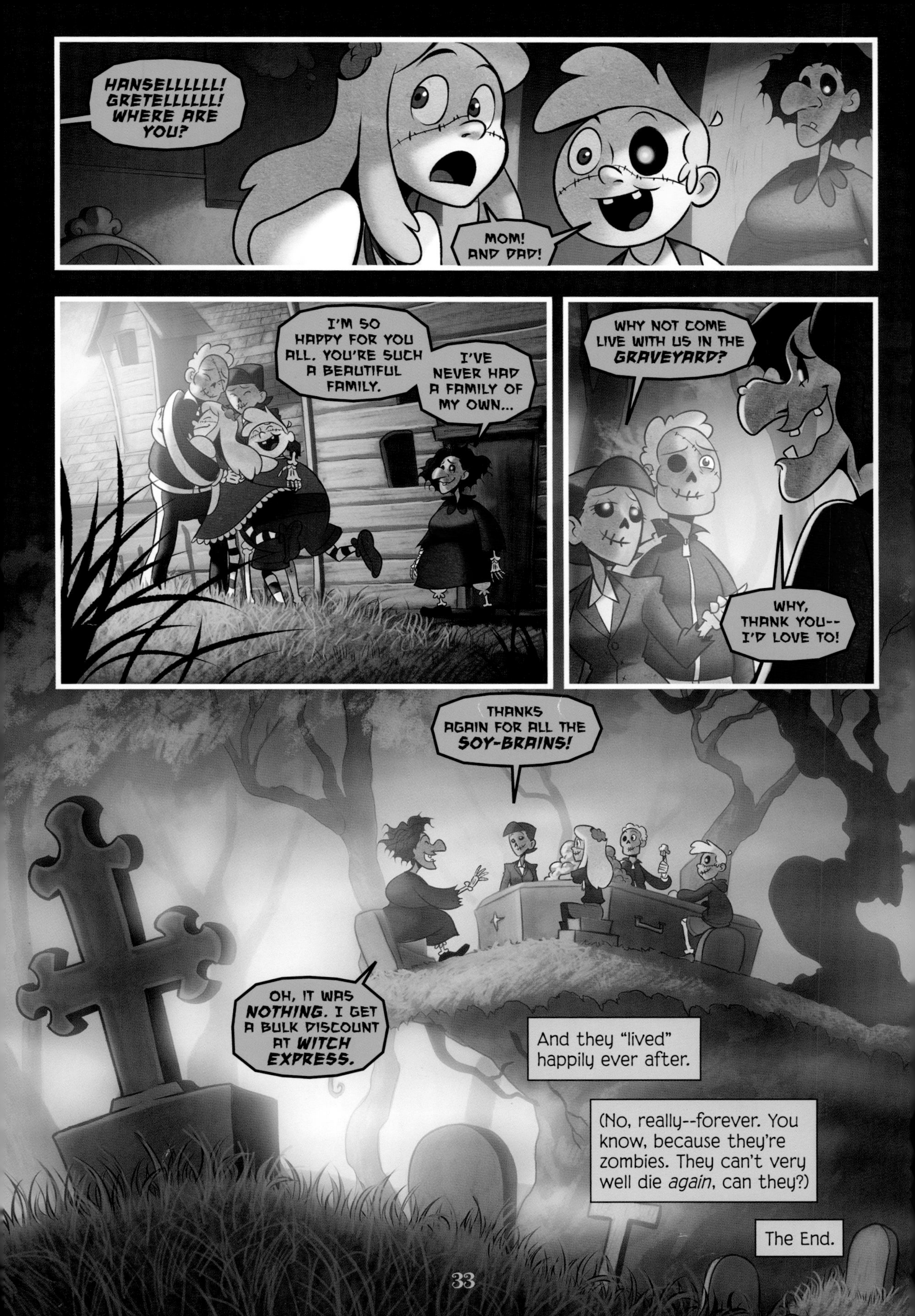
HANSELLLLLL! GRETELLLLLL! WHERE ARE YOU?
MOM! AND DAD!
I'M SO HAPPY FOR YOU ALL. YOU'RE SUCH A BEAUTIFUL FAMILY.
I'VE NEVER HAD A FAMILY OF MY OWN...
WHY NOT COME LIVE WITH US IN THE GRAVEYARD?
WHY, THANK YOU-- I'D LOVE TO!
THANKS AGAIN FOR ALL THE SOY-BRAINS!
OH, IT WAS NOTHING. I GET A BULK DISCOUNT AT WITCH EXPRESS.
And they "lived" happily ever after.
(No, really--forever. You know, because they're zombies. They can't very well die again, can they?)
The End.

ALL ABOUT THE ORIGINAL TALE!

Zombies didn't appear in the original Brothers Grimm version of "Hansel and Gretel." However, Hansel and Gretel's parents were pretty *monstrous*.

You see, they tried not once--but twice--to abandon their children in the forest so they couldn't return home. The parents succeeded the second time, leaving Hansel and Gretel lost in the woods. In fact, their mother was so monstrous that she led them even farther into the woods, ensuring they would never find their way home.

Lost and alone in the woods, Hansel and Gretel wandered aimlessly until they felt the need to lay down and sleep. Several days passed like this, until they grew so hungry they could scarcely bear it. However, they soon came upon a strange sight: a house's walls made entirely of bread, and the roof was made of cakes and other sweets.

The siblings, desperately hungry at this point, started snacking on the gingerbread house. Soon, the house's owner spotted them and welcomed them inside. To their surprise, the woman turned out to be a hungry witch who eats children!

The witch plumped up Hansel, hoping to make him nice and fat so he would be a bigger meal for her to eat. Meanwhile, the witch forced Gretel to work--and fed her nothing but crab shells.

One morning, the witch told Gretel to climb inside the hot oven to see if it was warm enough to bake bread. Gretel knew the witch was up to something, so she asked her to climb inside instead--and kicked the witch into the oven. She was never seen again.

Gretel freed her brother. In a room next to the kitchen, they found boxes of precious gems! When they finally found their way home, they discovered their father alone. While they'd been gone, their evil mother had died. Gretel tugged on her apron, releasing all the gems. The three of them lived richly and happily ever after.

A FAR OUT GUIDE TO HANSEL & GRETEL'S TALE TWISTS

Two innocent, human siblings star in the original tale. In this version, they're zombies!

Hansel & Gretel get nabbed by the witch when they nibble on her house. Zombie Hansel & Gretel get kidnapped because they *won't* eat the candy-house!

In the original tale, a witch tries to eat the children, but they burn her to cinders. (Yikes!) In this book, Zombie Gretel bites the witch, transforming her into one of them!

In the Brothers Grimm versi of the story, the mother an the witch die. But in this far out version, everyone lives happily ever after--even the witch!

ISUAL QUESTIONS

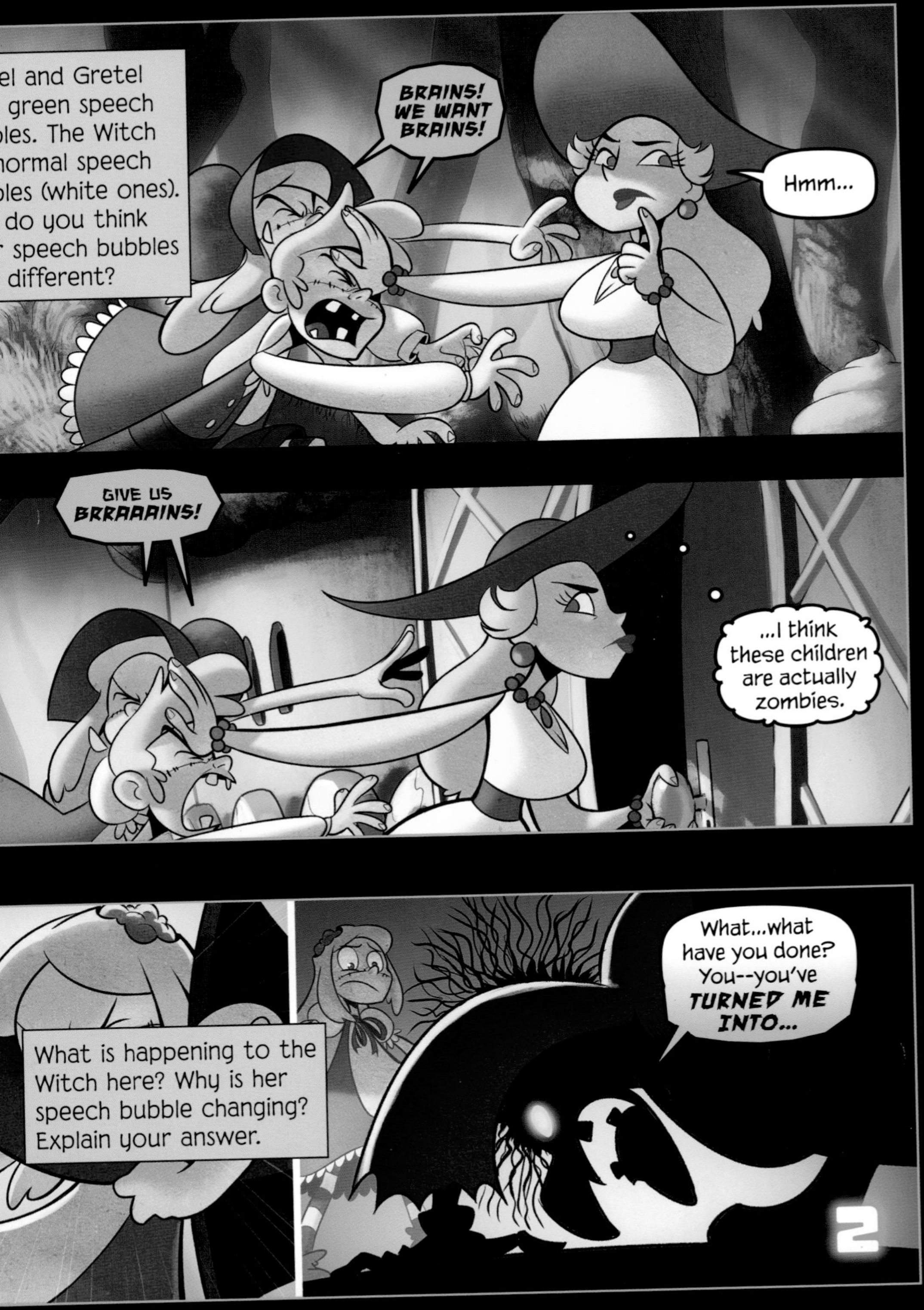

el and Gretel green speech bles. The Witch normal speech bles (white ones). do you think r speech bubbles different?
BRAINS! WE WANT BRAINS!
Hmm...
GIVE US BRRAAAINS!
...I think these children are actually zombies.
What is happening to the Witch here? Why is her speech bubble changing? Explain your answer.
What...what have you done? You--you've TURNED ME INTO...
2

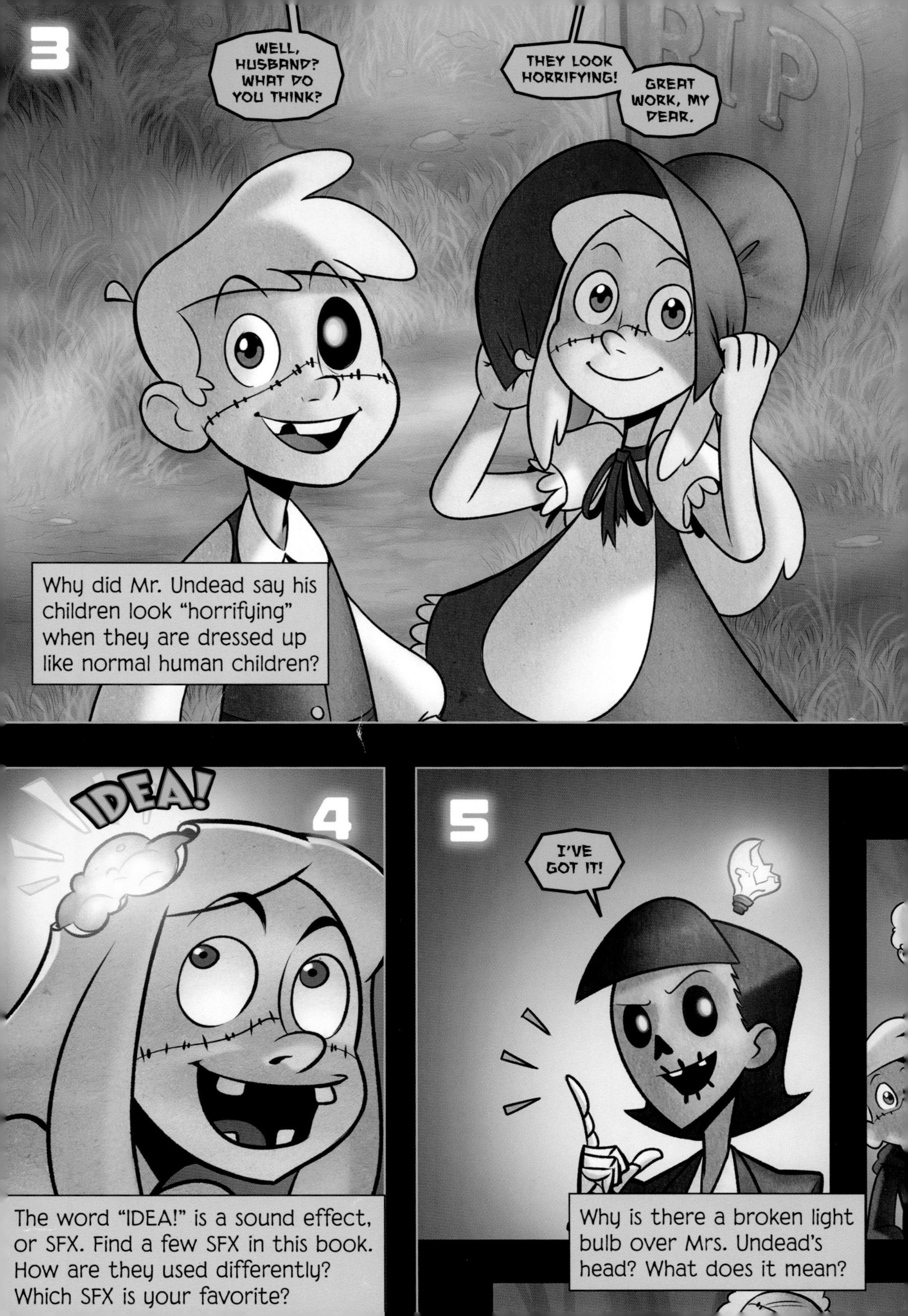
3
WELL, HUSBAND? WHAT DO YOU THINK?
THEY LOOK HORRIFYING!
GREAT WORK, MY DEAR.
RIP
Why did Mr. Undead say his children look “horrifying” when they are dressed up like normal human children?
IDEA!
4
The word “IDEA!” is a sound effect, or SFX. Find a few SFX in this book. How are they used differently? Which SFX is your favorite?
5
I'VE GOT IT!
Why is there a broken light bulb over Mrs. Undead's head? What does it mean?

AUTHOR

Benjamin Harper has worked as an editor at Lucasfilm LTD. and DC Comics. He currently works at Warner Bros. Consumer Products in Burbank, California. He has written many books, including *Obsessed With Star Wars* and *Thank You, Superman!*

ILLUSTRATOR

Fernandó Cano is an illustrator born in Mexico City, Mexico. He currently resides in Monterrey, Mexico, where he makes a living as an illustrator and colorist. He has done work for Marvel, DC Comics, and role-playing games like Pathfinder from Paizo Publishing. In his spare time, he enjoys hanging out with friends, singing, rowing, and drawing!

GLOSSARY

abandoned (uh-BAN-duhnd)--left behind without needed protection or care

character (KAYR-ik-tur)--if someone is playing a character, they pretend to be someone other than who they are

goiter (GOY-ter)--a swelling on the front of the neck

horrifying (HAWR-uh-fye-ing)--causing someone to feel horror, shock, or upset

journey (JUR-nee)--an act of traveling from one place to another, often to an undetermined location

soy (SOY)--soybeans and the food products that are made from soybeans. Many vegetarian foods are made from soy.

undead (uhn-DED)--no longer alive but still able to move around

urchins (UR-chinz)--an old-fashioned name for children that are poor, dirty, annoying, or likely to cause trouble

vulnerable (VUHL-ner-uh-buhl)--easily hurt or harmed physically, mentally, or emotionally

zombie (ZOM-bee)--a dead person who is able to move because of magical means

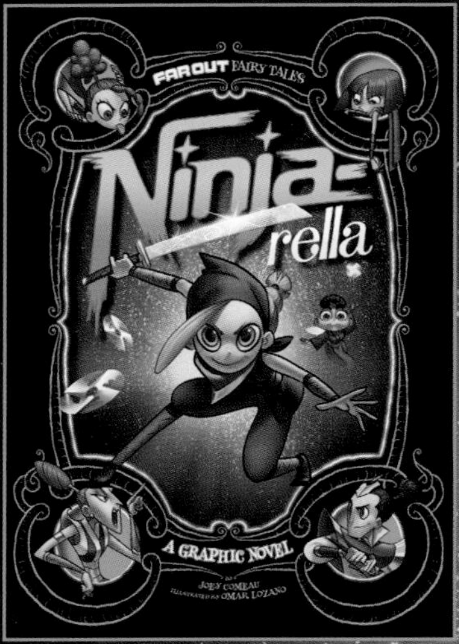
FAR OUT FAIRY TALES
Ninja-rella
A GRAPHIC NOVEL

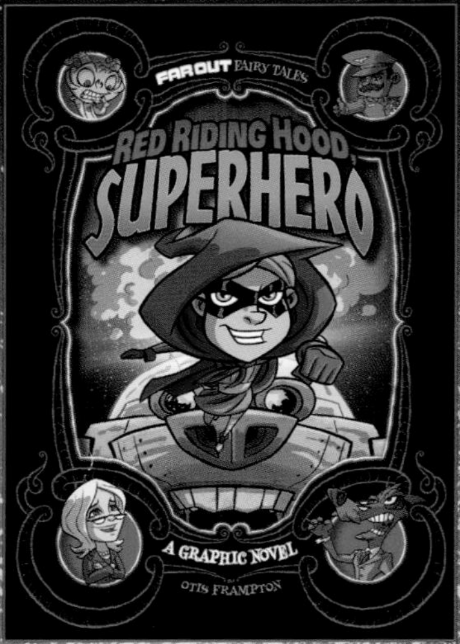
FAR OUT FAIRY TALES
RED RIDING HOOD SUPERHERO
A GRAPHIC NOVEL
OTIS FRAMPTON

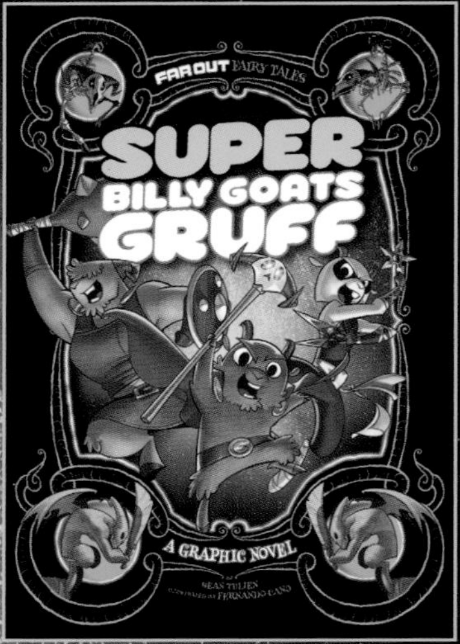
FAR OUT FAIRY TALES
SUPER BILLY GOATS GRUFF
A GRAPHIC NOVEL

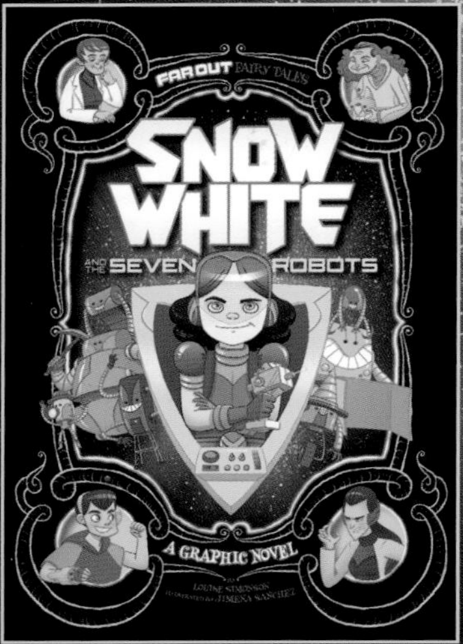
FAR OUT FAIRY TALES
SNOW WHITE AND THE SEVEN ROBOTS
A GRAPHIC NOVEL

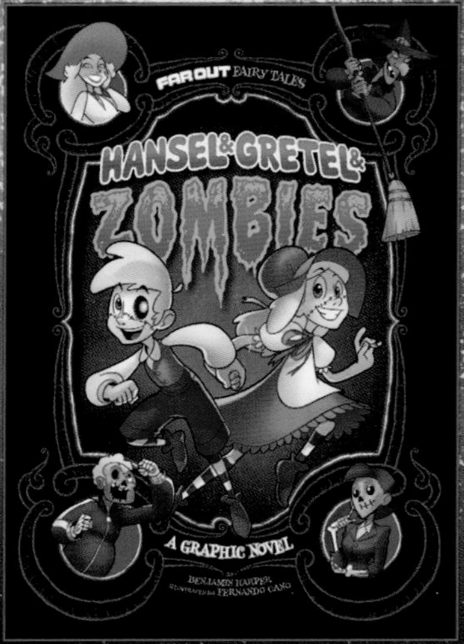
FAR OUT FAIRY TALES
HANSEL & GRETEL & ZOMBIES
A GRAPHIC NOVEL

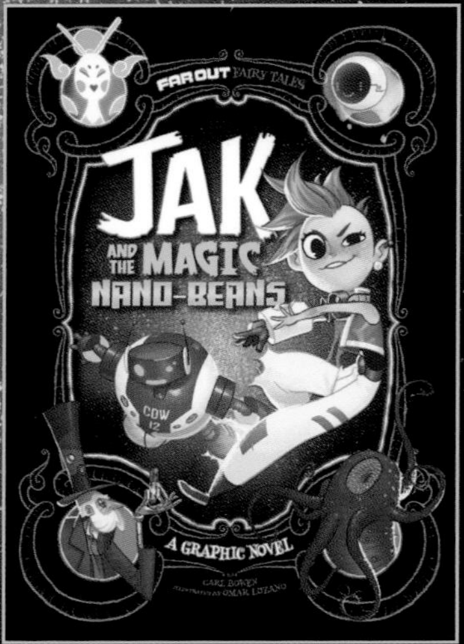
FAR OUT FAIRY TALES
JAK AND THE MAGIC NANO-BEANS
A GRAPHIC NOVEL